Ψ

"Close your eyes.

Sean did. He felt a rush of cold air, as if someone had opened the door.

"You can open them," she said.

He stared out the front door at a horse-drawn sleigh in his driveway. A large black horse pulled a red-and-green sleigh decorated with garlands. Two old-fashioned lanterns hung off the front. A driver with a stovepipe hat in forest-green held the reins with gloved hands.

Zoë touched her lips gently to his. "Merry Christmas, Sean."

"Wow. I never would have expected this."

She pulled back to gaze into his eyes, hers wide with hope. "You like it?"

"I love it."

I love you, he thought. But he wasn't ready to say the words just yet.

Dear Reader,

You know how certain people intrigue you? How some places draw you back again and again? That happened to me writing about Sean Hughes and Hood Hamlet, Oregon.

Both first appeared in *Rescued by the Magic of Christmas*. I fell in love with the quaint mountain town, and I wanted to give the handsome team leader of Oregon Mountain Search and Rescue his own story.

My original idea had heartbreaker Sean and his loyal Siberian husky rescuing my injured heroine. I submitted a brief story line to my editor and was good to go. And then I heard from the sister of a friend about Michael Leming, a member of Portland Mountain Rescue and one of my go-to guys for research questions.

Michael had been climbing a twelve-foot vertical piece of ice just below the summit of Mount Hood. A chunk had sheared off. He fell back on a fifty-degree slope and slid over two hundred feet. He was taken off the mountain by helicopter with two injured ankles.

Fortunately Michael's injuries weren't life threatening, but he did require rehab and physical therapy. Thirteen weeks later, however, he climbed Mount Hood—a tad slowly—and snowboarded down from 9,500 feet. A year after his accident his ankles are at ninety percent.

Once I knew Michael would be okay, the writer in me took over. I kept thinking about a rescuer needing to be rescued. Suddenly I knew I had to change my story. The changes kept getting better when my editor asked me if I could set the story during Christmastime.

I had so much fun writing about Sean Hughes and Zoë Flynn Carrington and revisiting Hood Hamlet. It's a story about hope, family and of course love!

Enjoy.

Melissa

MELISSA McCLONE

Christmas Magic on the Mountain

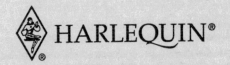

HARLEQUIN®

TORONTO • NEW YORK • LONDON
AMSTERDAM • PARIS • SYDNEY • HAMBURG
STOCKHOLM • ATHENS • TOKYO • MILAN • MADRID
PRAGUE • WARSAW • BUDAPEST • AUCKLAND

Recycling programs for this product may not exist in your area.

ISBN-13: 978-0-373-17694-6

CHRISTMAS MAGIC ON THE MOUNTAIN

First North American Publication 2010

Copyright © 2010 by Melissa Martinez McClone

With a degree in mechanical engineering from Stanford University, the last thing **Melissa McClone** ever thought she would be doing was writing romance novels. But analyzing engines for a major U.S. airline just couldn't compete with her "happily-ever-afters." When she isn't writing, caring for her three young children or doing laundry, Melissa loves to curl up on the couch with a cup of tea, her cats and a good book. She enjoys watching home decorating shows to get ideas for her house—a 1939 cottage that is *slowly* being renovated. Melissa lives in Lake Oswego, Oregon, with her own real-life hero husband, two daughters, a son, two lovable but oh-so-spoiled indoor cats and a no-longer-stray outdoor kitty that decided to call the garage home. Melissa loves to hear from her readers. You can write to her at P.O. Box 63, Lake Oswego, OR 97034, U.S.A., or contact her via her website, www.melissamcclone.com.

For Virginia Kantra, my critique partner
extraordinaire, and Michael Leming,
who patiently answers all my questions.

Special thanks to Erik Denninghoff, M.D.,
Brook Holter PA-C, John Frieh, Porter Hammer
and Steve Rollins. Any mistakes and/or
discrepancies are entirely the author's fault.

CHAPTER ONE

THE FAMILIAR sound of the crunch of traction tires against packed snow filled the cab of Sean Hughes's truck. He inhaled the crisp air laced with the scent of pine and the smell of wet dog. Denali, his Siberian husky, panted on the seat next to him.

Winter on Mount Hood was their favorite time of year—boarding, climbing and snowshoeing. Sean grimaced wryly. Too bad Thanksgiving and Christmas had to get in the way of all that fun.

A snowplow heading west passed him.

No doubt the early morning road crews working hard to clear the overnight snowfall from Highway 26. Portlanders would be driving up in throngs today to spend Thanksgiving on the slopes or eating turkey at Timberline Lodge's Cascade dining room.

Sean wished he could be one of them.

A well-cooked dinner served by an obliging wait staff at a nice restaurant where quiet conversation was de rigueur would be better than the chaotic holiday meal at his parents' house where everyone poked their noses into everybody's business. Especially his. No one listened to his "let's eat dinner out" suggestion—not even when he offered to pay for all thirty-eight of them. Make that thirty-nine. One of his cousins had given birth to another baby a couple of months ago.

"A good thing we don't have to be at Mom and Dad's until later." Sean glanced at Denali. "I'd rather spend this bluebird day on the mountain than be stuck inside listening to people tell me what's missing from my life is a wife."

Denali nudged his arm with her nose.

"They don't seem to understand you're my number one girl." Sean patted the dog's head. He had nothing against marriage per se, but he didn't have the time necessary to make a relationship work. He had too many other things going on in his life to make any woman a priority. In the past, he'd somehow given women the wrong idea about his commitment level so now he only dated casually. Much to his family's dismay. "No worries. We'll make the most of the time we have on our own this morning."

The dog stared out the windshield and barked.

At the base of the road leading up to Timberline Lodge stood a snowboarder. A large, overstuffed backpack set at his feet along with a board.

Around here, no one thought twice about hitchhiking up to the ski area or giving a skier or snowboarder a lift.

Sean remembered hitching rides up the hill from locals and strangers when he'd been a teenager. Back then he'd worked all summer for his dad to pay for a season pass. He'd pack a lunch since he couldn't afford to buy a cup of hot chocolate, let alone food. Times and his circumstances sure had changed since then. But seeing the kid made Sean remember the joy and freedom of those days.

Flicking on his left turn signal, he tapped the brakes to slow down. The image of the kid hoping for a ride made a great visual. He would have to mention that to the advertising firm his snowboard manufacturing company used. They were already talking about next season's promo campaign.

He turned off the highway, pulled over to the right and rolled down the passenger window.

A burst of frigid air rushed in. Denali stuck her head out.

The snowboarder straightened. "Hi."

Not a kid. A woman. Even better.

"Hey," Sean said to her.

A wool beanie hid her hair. The fit of her jacket made him wonder what curves lay underneath.

"Beautiful dog," she said.

"Thanks." The woman was pretty herself with pink cheeks and glossed lips. Her outerwear coordinated with the graphics on her board. Not one of his snowboards, but she looked like the type of rider more interested in fashion than in function. He didn't mind. Sean had a soft spot for snow bunnies, especially ones who boarded. "Heading up for a taste of the fresh powder?"

"I hear it's light and fluffy. My favorite kind." Hopeful, clear blue eyes fringed with thick lashes met his. "Have room for one more?"

She was young. Early twenties, maybe. But cute. Very cute. She'd be turning some heads on the slopes today the way she had turned his.

He shifted the truck's gear stick into Park. "I'll put your stuff in the back."

A wide smile lit up her face. "Thanks, but I've got it."

Independent. Sean liked that. Much better than the women who wanted him to do everything for them.

In the rearview mirror, he watched as she put her things into the back. He appreciated how careful she was to avoid his splitboard and the prototype bindings he'd been working on. She kicked the snow from her boots, climbed in the cab and closed the door.

"I can't tell you how happy I am you stopped." She pulled off her mittens and wiggled her fingers in front of the dashboard vents. "Oh, the heat feels so good."

She smelled good. Like vanilla. He wouldn't mind seeing if she tasted as good as she smelled. "Been waiting long?"

"It felt like forever." Her fingers fumbled with the seat belt until she managed to fasten it. "But it was probably only twenty minutes or so. There isn't as much traffic as I thought there'd be this morning."

"Most people won't head up until later." He shifted gears,

pressed on the gas pedal and drove up the curving road to Timberline Lodge. "The lifts don't open until nine."

"That explains it." She rubbed her hands together. "I'm Zoe."

"Sean Hughes." Walls of snow from the plow lined each side of the road. "This is Denali."

"Nice to meet both of you."

Denali rubbed her muzzle against Zoe's cheek.

"Off," Sean ordered, his gaze focusing for a moment on Zoe's high cheekbones. The dog obeyed. "She's very friendly."

"I see that." Zoe glanced at the window behind them. "I noticed an OMSAR sticker on the window."

"Oregon Mountain Search and Rescue."

She fiddled with her mittens on her lap. "You guys are on TV a lot."

"When something happens on the mountain, the media flock to Timberline, but otherwise they pretty much leave us alone."

"I suppose really bad things happen up there."

"Sometimes." He thought about fellow OMSAR member and good friend Nick Bishop who had died almost seven years ago climbing on the Reid Headwall. "Accidents can happen to the best climbers."

"I'd like to climb a mountain someday."

"There isn't much in this world that beats standing on a summit," he encouraged. "But it's all about getting to the top and back down safely. You need to be ready, prepared."

With a nod, she rested her left hand on a contented-looking Denali.

Sean noticed her bare ring finger. He'd bet she had a boyfriend. Still, awareness buzzed through him.

"Before I forget," she said. "Happy Thanksgiving."

"Same to you." At least Thanksgiving was only one day. That made the holiday a hundred percent better than Christmas, when the chorus of "When are you settling down?"

questions drowned out the carols from the stereo. "You're not from around here."

She stiffened. "Why do you say that?"

"A local would know what time the lifts open."

"Oh, right."

Her cheeks remained pink, even though it wasn't cold in the truck. The women he went out with rarely blushed, but Sean found it charming.

"I got a ride up from Portland yesterday and spent the night at the Hood Hamlet Hostel. I wanted to get an early start this morning." She rubbed Denali. "Spending the day on the slopes before Thanksgiving dinner is a family tradition, but I think I may have started a little too early. I suppose getting up before the sun should have been a clue."

He smiled. "Are you meeting your family later?"

"No." She stared out the window. "I'm on my own this year."

Interesting. Maybe there wasn't a boyfriend in the picture. At least not a serious one.

"Lucky you." Sean negotiated the truck around a tight curve. "I wish I were on my own today."

Zoe turned toward him, her eyes wide. "But it's Thanksgiving."

He smiled. "Exactly."

"The holidays are a time to spend with family."

"I know," he admitted. "That's why I'll be at my parents' house this afternoon with more than three dozen extended family members. Picture total chaos with cooking in the kitchen, football blaring on the TV in the living room, kids running around screaming and my uncle Marty snoring in the recliner. It's so crazy, you can't keep track of the score of the game."

"It sounds wonderful to me."

Zoe sounded wistful, a little sad. Maybe she wasn't as keen on spending Thanksgiving by herself as he would be. Sean couldn't deny his attraction. Truth was, he wouldn't mind spending time with her. "You want to come?"

Uncertainty filled her eyes. "I don't know you."

"You want references? I can probably get 'em for you."

"I know."

He looked at her, not understanding what she meant.

"The OMSAR sticker," she explained. "And you gave me a lift. Obviously you're used to rescuing damsels in distress."

"Rescue is my specialty." That earned him a smile. "So dinner?"

She shook her head.

"Is it my family? Because my relatives make me nuts, but not in an ax-murderer kind of way. The rugrats are pretty cute, and the pies are really good. Ask anyone at the ski area about the Hughes family. We've lived in Hood Hamlet forever."

She laughed, as he hoped she would. "No, I meant... You can't spring an unexpected guest on your mother at the last minute."

Pretty and polite. Not too shabby. "My mom lives for holidays. She makes enough food to send leftovers home with everyone, including Denali."

"That's really kind of you, but—"

"You have other plans."

"No," she said. "I wouldn't want to impose."

"You wouldn't."

"Last-minute guests are always impositions."

Sean should let it go, except he didn't want to. He could tell she was considering his invitation. She obviously didn't want to be on her own for the holiday. He didn't want her to be alone, either.

Besides, he was the last unmarried cousin. His relatives close to his age, some much younger, were all chasing after kids or holding babies now. He didn't have anything in common with them anymore. It had been his choice to remain single, and he really did enjoy his lifestyle—running a successful company, boarding, climbing, mountain rescue. But a part of Sean felt as if he'd been left behind, and his cousins—make that all of his relatives—were trying to get him to catch up.

Bringing home a pretty girl in need of a family Thanksgiving dinner tonight would not only help her, but deflect the personal questions about his sex life from male relatives, and questions about who he'd been seeing from the female ones.

"It'll be fine." Dinner at his folks' would be good for Zoe's morale. His, too. "You can ask my mom yourself."

"No, I couldn't."

"Then I will."

Zoe stared at him. "Do you really feel comfortable inviting a total stranger to have Thanksgiving dinner with your family?"

He didn't want to explain how her presence would take the heat off him or how being with Zoe might actually make tonight fun instead of a chore. If things went well during dinner, maybe they could spend more time together afterward. At his house. Alone. "I can take you if you pull any funny stuff."

"You think?"

Sean's blood pressure spiked. He'd been around the block enough times to know when a woman was interested. Zoe was. Her flirting suggested tonight would turn out way better than he'd thought when he woke up this morning.

"Definitely." He flashed her one of his most charming smiles, the one that had melted his share of female hearts. "Besides, one of my cousins is married to a sheriff's deputy, and another is a martial arts instructor. You wouldn't stand a chance against us."

She laughed. "No funny stuff, I promise."

"So you're in."

"Only if it's okay with your mom."

Sean didn't want Zoe to change her mind. He hit the button on his cell phone and called his parents' number. His mother answered on the second ring with a cheerful "gobble, gobble."

"Hey, Mom, I'm bringing someone with me to dinner tonight. Okay?"

"Honey, you know your friends are always welcome," she said. "We have more than enough food."

"Thanks. I'll tell her."

"Her?" His mother's voice shot up an octave. "You're bringing a girl?"

"Her name's Zoe. She's going to be boarding at T-line while I'm up on the hill trying out a new binding."

"And then you're bringing her home for Thanksgiving dinner. That's wonderful, Sean. Of course Zoe's welcome to come."

Something about his mother's tone set off alarm bells in the back of his head. "I don't want you making a big deal out of this and scaring her off, Mom."

His mother laughed. "Of course not. I'll be discreet, I promise. Let me talk to her."

He frowned and looked over at Zoe. "She wants to talk to you."

A puzzled expression crossed Zoe's face. "Me?"

"Maybe she wants to give you references," he joked.

"Hello?" Zoe said into the phone, almost shyly. "Yes, this is Zoe...Zoe Flynn... Thank you, Mrs. Hughes. Okay, Connie... No, my family isn't... I've been out here on my own for a while...."

The way she spoke made Sean smile. He knew his mom's interrogation skills all too well, but Zoe was holding her own when she could get a word in. He was curious to see how she handled everyone at the dinner tonight.

"Yes, holidays are hard alone," she said. "I appreciate it... I understand. I just didn't want Sean to spring an extra guest on you at the last minute.... Yes, he is.... Thanks again.... I look forward to meeting you, too.... Yes. Yes, I'll tell him."

Zoe handed the phone back to him. "Here you go."

He was about to say goodbye, but the line was already disconnected. His mother had hung up. That was...odd.

He tucked the phone in his pocket, both relieved and puzzled. "What are you suppose to tell me?"

Zoe drew her eyebrows together. "Your mother wants me to remind you about your grandmother's present. It's in the safe-deposit box. She said she could pick it up from the bank for you on Monday morning."

His grandmother's present. His grandmother's...

"Oh, hell," Sean said.

"What is it?" Zoe asked.

His grandmother's engagement ring, intended for Sean's future bride. And now his mother thought... His mother planned...

"Damn. She thinks it's serious."

"Your grandmother? Is she ill?"

"She's dead," he explained. "No, it's my mother. She thinks we're serious. You and me. That I invited you to dinner because we're in a relationship."

Lines creased Zoe's forehead. "Why would she think that?"

Because his mother was a hopeless romantic who wanted her son to get married so she could have grandchildren. "Because I'm bringing you to Thanksgiving dinner."

"That doesn't make any sense."

"My family never makes much sense."

"Haven't you ever brought anyone to Thanksgiving dinner before?" Zoe asked.

"Not in a long time." Sean tried to keep his personal life as private as he could. Not easy living in a nosy, small town full of close friends and a large, demanding family. "That must be how she got the wrong idea."

"You have to admit it's kind of sweet."

"Imagine if it was your mother."

Zoe winced. "Okay, not sweet at all."

"My mom's probably calling my aunts who will call my cousins..."

"It's not a problem, Sean. It's just a little misunderstanding." Zoe smiled. "We can tell everyone the truth when we arrive and have a good laugh about it."

He stared at the snow on the side of the road. "Right."

"You're not laughing," she said gently.

"Nope."

"I don't have to go," Zoe offered.

"You're not spending Thanksgiving alone." Sean wasn't going to let her get away that easily. He blew out a puff of air. "My mom's expecting you now. It would disappoint her if you didn't show up. She looks forward to the holidays all year. I don't want to ruin her day."

"She's going to be disappointed anyway when we tell her the truth."

"Yeah."

"Unless…" Zoe's voice trailed off.

"What?"

"We could pretend to be dating," she suggested. "Just for today."

That would solve his problem. Problems, actually. His mom's Thanksgiving would be salvaged, his opinionated family would be off his back about settling down and he would get to spend time with Zoe. A win-win situation for everyone.

"Bad idea?" Zoe asked.

Probably.

"No." He liked that she was both helpful and a little daring. He also liked the idea of what might happen while she was playing his girlfriend. "But it's a lot for me to ask. Are you up for it?"

"I know what it's like to disappoint your family."

The sincerity in Zoe's voice covered him like a soft, warm quilt. He wasn't used to a woman making him feel like that. It made him…uncomfortable.

Still, she was willing. Why not? "I owe you."

"You gave me a lift up here, and I get a free Thanksgiving dinner out of the deal." Zoe smiled. "I'd say we're even."

Not even close once she met his crazy family, but he'd make sure she had a good time. At dinner and afterward. He grinned. "Okay, thanks."

"You're welcome."

Funny, but Sean was looking forward to Thanksgiving for the first time in years.

They arrived at Timberline. The lot was almost empty. He parked the truck close to the WyEast day lodge and turned off the engine.

"Would you mind if I leave my pack in the cab?" Zoe asked. "It would save me paying the locker fee."

"Not a problem." That was the least he could do for her. "Denali and I are going to head up the mountain a ways so I can try out some new bindings. You want to come?

"Thanks, but resort runs are more my speed."

He was unexpectedly disappointed she wasn't up for it. He liked being with her. "I can hang with you down here."

"I'll just slow you down," she said. "Have fun riding the freshiez up top. I'll see you later."

Sean wanted to see how his new design performed, and he didn't want to push her too much. He would have plenty of time to charm her later at the Thanksgiving dinner. "Okay."

She reached for the door handle. "When should we meet back here?"

"Two o'clock," he answered. "That will give us plenty of time to get to my parents' house."

"Sounds good, but this is my first day out this season." Zoe looked up at the summit. He followed her line of sight. The snowcapped peak contrasted sharply against the blue sky. "I might be finished before then."

"Do you want my cell phone number?" he asked.

"I don't have a phone with me."

"I'll leave the keys on the top of the rear left tire so you can get into the cab whenever you want."

"Thanks." She studied him. "It's not often you meet some-one who is so trusting of strangers."

"I could say the same about you."

"Yes."

"But don't forget you're not a stranger," he said playfully. "You're my Thanksgiving-day girlfriend."

She grinned. "Mustn't forget that."

Sean sure wouldn't. He was really looking forward to tonight. "Besides you don't look like the type who would steal her boyfriend's truck."

"What type do I look like?" she asked.

Sean gave her the once-over.

She dressed the part of a snow bunny, but with her cap pulled down over her hair and little to no makeup on her face, she had the fresh-faced-girl-next-door look down. Sean didn't normally go for that type, but something about Zoe intrigued him. Still he didn't want to appear too interested. He was imposing on her enough already.

He smiled. "You look like the type of girlfriend a guy brings home to meet the family."

Around a quarter to two, Zoe Flynn Carrington made her way past the WyEast day lodge toward the parking lot. Her muscles ached from all the snowboarding. Even though she'd had fun on the slopes, she kind of regretted not taking Sean up on his offer to go up the mountain with him.

Thinking about his thoughtful hazel-green eyes, easy smile and the brown strands of hair poking out from under his ski hat warmed her cold insides right up.

A mountain rescuer to the rescue. Zoe grinned.

She couldn't wait to see him again.

The guy was gorgeous—a yummy piece of eye candy who would fit into one of the trendy new hotspots in L.A. as well as he did here on the mountain. He probably had women throwing themselves at him. Yet she got to be his girlfriend for the rest of the day.

Anticipation rippled through her.

He seemed as interested in flirting with her as she was with him on the drive up. Tonight could get interesting.

She felt an unfamiliar prick of caution.

Not interesting, Zoe corrected.

Her suggestion to be his pretend girlfriend had been nothing but impulsive, something she'd vowed not to be anymore. But the idea of having a home-cooked family Thanksgiving dinner tugged at her lonely heart, and the thought of spending more time with handsome Sean filled her tummy with tingles. She'd spoken without thinking. She hadn't been able to help herself even though she had no room in her life for romance at the moment.

Zoe located his truck in the now-full lot and made her way toward it.

She would have to be more careful, more vigilant. She couldn't afford not to be. Not that she was in any position to afford anything right now.

As she waited for an SUV to drive by so she could cross the road, her boots sank in the slush of melted snow.

With the end of the month approaching and her allowance almost gone, she'd only had enough money to do one of two things: buy a lift ticket or eat Thanksgiving dinner. Obviously she'd made the right choice because now she would get both.

Thanks to Sean Hughes.

With a smile pulling at her lips, she crossed the road.

Maybe her luck was finally changing.

What type do I look like?

You look like the type of girlfriend a guy brings home to meet the family.

She'd wanted to hug Sean for saying that, even if he might be the only person in the world who thought so. Maybe what she felt for him wasn't really attraction, but gratitude. Being with Sean made her feel different, better than she'd felt in a long time. A good thing since the past few months had been so bad, so hard on her.

Wild Child. Party Animal. Homewrecker.

She cringed at the memory of the tabloid headlines written about her. Headlines that everyone believed even though they were lies. Headlines that had ripped everyone she held dear from her. Headlines that had ruined her life.

You are an embarrassment to me, to your brothers and to the Carrington name. You need to learn responsibility. And I can think of only one way for that to happen.

Zoe sighed.

No matter. The past was behind her. She was on the other side of the country from her family. All she had to do was remain out of sight, stay away from the media spotlight and keep out of trouble until after the special election for the vacant U.S. Senate seat her mother, Governor Vanessa Carrington, wanted more than anything in the world.

If Zoe failed to do any of those three things, her mother, the executor of her father's will, would tie up Zoe's access to her trust fund until she was forty. Sixteen years from now. The same length of time her mother had been governor. Her mother was serving her fourth term and couldn't seek reelection, which explained her fixation on winning the Senate seat.

A dog barked.

Denali ran around the side of the truck and nearly knocked Zoe over with excitement.

"Hi, pretty girl." Zoe hugged the dog. "I missed you, too."

Denali panted. The dog's hot breath hanging in the air like little puffs of clouds.

Zoe placed her board in the back of Sean's truck. Funny, but she didn't see his board. That seemed weird. Especially since Denali had her leash on. Had Sean tied her to the truck? "Where's—?"

"You must be Zoe."

She cringed. With her helmet and goggles, no one should be able to recognize her. "I am."

A tall man wearing a black-and-red jacket with the initials OMSAR written in white on the front and Rescue on the sleeves held on to the end of Denali's leash. "Jake Porter. I'm a friend of Sean's."

She raised her goggles onto the front of her helmet.

Intense blue eyes stared down at her. Like Sean, he wore a ski hat, and that emphasized his ruggedly handsome features. He wasn't as gorgeous as Sean, but he was still good-looking. Were all mountain rescuers hotties?

Speaking of which… She glanced around the parking lot. "Where is he?"

"There's been an accident."

"Oh, no." She touched Denali's head. "I saw a helicopter earlier and wondered if someone had been injured. Is Sean helping out?"

"Sean's been hurt."

"Sean?" Zoe's stomach clenched. Her hand dropped to her side. "How?"

"He fell."

Accidents can happen to the best of climbers.

A chill inched its way down her spine. "Is he okay?"

Jake looked at Denali. "He was unconscious when he was found, but was conscious when we placed him in a vacuum splint to immobilize his spine."

She trembled. "His spine?"

"We do that as a precaution. With his head injury we couldn't clear his cervical spine of injury."

A head injury sounded really serious. Really bad. "Did he hurt anything else?"

Jake hesitated.

"Please," she urged.

"His left leg is broken. We couldn't tell if his right ankle is or not," Jake explained. "Fortunately, he was lower on the mountain so easier to reach. The rescue happened a lot quicker than normal. He should be at the hospital in Portland by now."

Sean had seemed so vibrant, so strong this morning. Zoe couldn't imagine him lying helpless on the snow unconscious. She shivered. "I can't believe he was the one in the helicopter. Have you called his parents?"

Jake nodded. "Hank and Connie are on their way to the hospital. She wants me to drive you there."

Connie. His mom. Who thought Zoe was Sean's serious girlfriend. And now Sean was seriously injured.

Zoe felt light-headed.

Jake touched her arm. "You're pale."

"I'm…" She wasn't fine, that was for certain. She only prayed Sean would be okay.

"This has to be a shock," Jake said compassionately.

No kidding. She took a deep breath.

"We should head out," he added.

She didn't know what to say. Going to the hospital seemed like a really bad idea. She was supposed to stay out of trouble, not dive headfirst into it. But what else could she do?

Zoe reached under his truck, removed the keys from the top of the left rear tire and handed them to Jake.

She wanted to know how Sean was doing. No way could she leave him in the lurch after he'd come to her rescue at the side of the road this morning. She remembered his not wanting to disappoint his mother and upset her plans for Thanksgiving.

Now he was in the hospital, and Zoe felt as if she had to take care of this for him. She would have to explain to his worried mother their supposed relationship was all a big joke.

Oh, dear.

Zoe's heart lodged in her throat.

Talk about a ruined Thanksgiving…

CHAPTER TWO

MOUNT HOOD lay far behind Zoe. Each passing mile brought her closer to the hospital, closer to Sean. He'd been on her mind for the past hour and twenty minutes. No matter how hard she tried, she couldn't stop thinking about him.

"We're almost there," Jake said from behind the wheel of Sean's truck.

Seeing the hospital's emergency department sign, she scrunched her mittens in her hand. Her concern over Sean doubled, but she was also a little worried about what she'd gotten herself into. How was she going to explain to his family that she didn't belong here with them? With Sean?

"This hospital has one of the best trauma centers in the Pacific Northwest," Jake said over Denali, who sat between them.

Zoe swallowed around the lump of fear in her throat. At least Sean was in good hands. "Thanks for driving me down here."

"Anything for Sean." Jake parked, cracked the windows and turned off the ignition. "I'll put your board in here."

As he opened the door, she looked down at the dog that stared back at her with big, reproachful eyes. Zoe bit her lip. "Um...what about Denali?"

"She'll be fine in the truck. It's cool enough for her. I'll bring her some water."

Zoe didn't know a lot about dogs, but that sounded good

to her. The dog seemed to mean a lot to Sean. She patted Denali's head.

Jake placed her snowboard in the cab and shut the door.

"Everything's going to be fine," Zoe said to the dog. She hoped. She would just get an update on Sean and tell his family...tell his family...

Denali nudged her arm.

"Stay," Zoe said firmly, remembering the way Sean had spoken to the dog on the drive up to Timberline.

The dog stayed.

Zoe glimpsed her board and backpack behind the front seat. She could grab both and be out of here in minutes. Seconds, really. She didn't have any real responsibility for Sean. Flirting aside, they were only tied by a crazy ruse they'd cooked up to satisfy his need for a holiday date to appease his mother and Zoe's need for a holiday family dinner to appease her heart.

Should she stay? Or go?

Zoe stared at the double-glass-door entrance to the emergency department. Apprehension shuddered through her. The last time she'd been to a hospital had been for her father. He'd gone in and never come out.

She remembered Sean's smile. The way laughter had lit his eyes.

Zoe had to stay. At least long enough to assure herself he would be all right. She forced herself out of the truck and closed the door.

Denali's sad stare followed Zoe accusingly as she backed away from the truck. Her breath hitched.

"Hang in there," Jake encouraged when he met her around the back of the pickup. "Sean's tough. Nothing will keep him down for long."

She knew nothing about Sean Hughes except he didn't seem to like his family's holiday get-togethers all that much. Still, she found herself nodding, hoping.

Zoe wanted Sean to be okay. He seemed like a good guy,

one who cared enough about his mother's feelings that he hadn't wanted to ruin her Thanksgiving.

"There could be a lot of Sean's family and friends here," Jake warned. "More will show up once the word gets out."

A close-knit group, she imagined. One of them would know she wasn't Sean's girlfriend, and if that person said something…anything to Sean's family before Zoe got the chance that would make matters worse.

Not that they weren't bad already.

She took a deep breath, trying to settle her already frayed nerves. It didn't help.

"Do you need anything from your pack?" Jake looked anxious, the way she felt. "Your purse?"

"No." Zoe shivered. From the chill in the air or cold feet, she didn't know. "We should probably get in there."

Even if it was the last place she wanted to be.

Jake nodded once.

The glass doors opened automatically. She stepped inside. Warm air surrounded her, yet she longed for the fresh, cold air outside.

On Zoe's right, a man sat behind a window. He took one look at Jake in his OMSAR jacket and waved them past. She walked through another set of doors.

The sterile, antiseptic hospital smell reminded Zoe painfully of her father's heart attack. Memories of being in the emergency room, waiting for word on her father's condition, brought a lump to her throat. She had sat on an uncomfortable chair, wishing she could see her father, but she'd never gotten that chance. He'd died surrounded by a team of medical professionals. Not family.

Zoe still regretted not being with her father at the end. But her father had been in his sixties, a victim of his lifestyle and diet choices. Sean was young, a victim of an accident. He might be a stranger, but she would help him if she could. The way she hadn't been able to help her dad.

She focused on the crowded waiting room in front of her.

The noise level surprised her. Conversations, commotion,

crying. A television set tuned to a twenty-four-hour news channel hung from one corner. Below it, a man coughed while a woman held his hand and comforted him. Next to them, a baby cried while a woman cradled her and rocked, humming a lullaby. Across from them, a teenager iced her ankle while a man paced near her.

In the opposite corner, a group of healthy-looking men and women filled seats while others stood. They spoke quietly amongst themselves, ignoring the chaos around them. The wide range of ages made Zoe think this had to be Sean's family and friends. All had one thing in common—worried expressions on their faces.

"That's Sean's family." Jake pointed to the group and led her over there. "Any word?"

"They've cleared his spine," a uniformed sheriff's deputy answered.

The relief on Jake's face matched the way Zoe felt inside. Now to find out about his head and his legs.

"They're doing a head CT now," the sheriff deputy added.

Tests were good, Zoe thought. Tests meant Sean was alive.

She noticed an OMSAR jacket hung on the back of one of the chairs.

A middle-aged woman, her brown hair sprinkled with gray, rose from one of the chairs. She wore a pumpkin-orange apron covered with pilgrims over her stylish brown pants and a chic matching tunic. She wiped at her red, swollen eyes with a tissue. "Zoe?"

The distress on the woman's face hurt Zoe's heart. She nodded.

"I'm Connie." Her slight smile faltered. "Sean's mom."

"I'm so sorry." Zoe didn't know what else to say.

Connie took a tentative step toward her.

Zoe did the same.

Suddenly she was enfolded in the woman's arms, engulfed in her warmth and the scent of cinnamon and cloves.

Connie let go. "When you love someone who lives to be in the mountains, you always know in the back of your mind this is a possibility, but the reality of it—"

The way the woman's voice cracked brought tears to Zoe's eyes.

"Sean's strong." He looked strong, so Zoe felt safe saying that much. "I'm sure he'll pull through this."

"You're right. I know you're right." Connie took a deep breath as if trying to compose herself. "Hank, Sean's dad, went to check with the nurse."

Zoe smiled. "Let's hope he has some good news to share."

Gratitude filled Connie's eyes. "Everyone, this is Sean's Zoe."

Oh, no. Zoe forced herself not to cringe as the group's attention focused on her and the temperature in the waiting area shot up by twenty degrees. Surely someone here would recognize her as a fraud.

Sweat trickled down Zoe's back, but her discomfort was nothing compared to what had happened to Sean. A few minutes of awkwardness over her and Sean being strangers was minor, nothing really, compared to what he and these people were going through right now.

She waited, but no one said a word. "Everyone" simply nodded as if they already knew who she was, as if being "Sean's Zoe" was enough for them.

People surrounded her. Names and hugs were exchanged like candy at Halloween. She kept waiting for someone to question her, to ask about her relationship with Sean, but no one did.

The sheriff's deputy handed her a cup of coffee.

"I'm Will Townsend," he introduced himself. "I'm married to Sean's cousin, Mary Sue. She and a couple others are at Connie and Hank's house cooking and watching kids." His cell phone rang. "Excuse me."

Zoe looked to see if anyone new had joined the group.

She wanted to know what Hank had found out about Sean's condition.

"I'm Leanne Thomas." A pretty but serious looking woman stepped forward. "I'm a friend of Sean's. I'm also a member of OMSAR and a paramedic. Right now they are doing a noncontrast head CT scan to see the extent of his head injury. Once that's done, they'll take X-rays of his legs and any other extremity where they might suspect an injury. We should get another update as soon as they're finished and can evaluate them."

"Waiting is the hardest part," Zoe said.

"You've been through this before."

The coffee cup warmed her cold hand. "With my dad."

"It never gets any easier, does it?" Leanne gave her a Hershey's candy bar. "I don't know about you, but chocolate always makes me feel better."

The woman was so nice. "Thanks."

Zoe stared at the candy bar. She was surprised at how anxious and worried she was to hear about Sean's condition. But receiving all this genuine sympathy from his friends and family made her feel lower than pond scum. They all thought Zoe cared because she was his girlfriend, because of a romantic attachment. She really needed to tell them the truth.

A middle-aged man she hadn't seen before walked toward her. He had the same athletic build and eyes as Sean, but lines of worry etched his face.

"I'm Hank, Sean's dad." His gaze rested on Connie, who was motioning to Zoe as she spoke with one of the OMSAR guys—Tim? No, maybe it was Bill.

"I'm sorry about Sean, Mr. Hughes," Zoe said sincerely.

"Hank," he corrected. "Don't worry about me. How are you holding up?"

"I'm fine." She was sweating from a combination of nerves and concern. She really should have stayed in the truck with Denali, but Zoe wanted to hear how Sean was doing. "Truly."

"Should have known Sean would pick himself a strong girl," Hank said approvingly.

She blinked. "No, I—"

"Let me tell you." He lowered his voice confidingly. "Connie was about to lose it before you arrived. Now she can fuss over you instead of sit here and worry until it makes her sick."

This is Sean's Zoe.

Guilt coated her mouth. Zoe hated deceiving these nice people, but they were so worried about Sean. She shouldn't—she couldn't—add to their troubles. That meant only one thing. She would have to be Sean's Zoe today.

Wrong, yes, but telling his family the truth when they were so upset seemed worse, even though their pretend relationship was nothing compared to Sean's injuries.

"I'm glad I'm here," she whispered. "Connie's free to fuss all she wants. Tell me what I can do to help, and I'll do it."

The corners of Hank's mouth curved. "You're going to fit right in."

That would be a first. Zoe smiled up at him.

An older, blue-haired woman, Aunt Vera if Zoe remembered correctly, studied her with an assessing gaze. "You're wearing snowboarding clothes and boots."

Zoe glanced down at her jacket, insulated cargo pants and boots. No wonder she felt so warm and was sweating. "I came straight from Timberline."

Unlike most of the others here. The OMSAR people were dressed for the mountains, but the Hughes men wore a mix of khakis and jeans. Long sleeved button-downs seemed to be the shirt of choice. The women wore dress pants or skirts with coordinating blouses. All were dressed for dinner. She obviously was not.

This wasn't the first time Zoe had been called out for what she was wearing. This wouldn't be the last once she returned home.

Home.

Thoughts of returning to her old life, partying with her

friends and using her Visa Platinum card had kept Zoe going these past weeks, but all that seemed suddenly foreign and empty compared to how these people were banding together over one of their own.

"Zoe has more on her mind than what she's wearing, Aunt Vera." Connie eyes softened when she looked at Zoe. "You must be burning up. Let me hold your coffee and candy so you can get rid of that jacket."

Zoe shrugged out of her jacket. She pulled off her ski cap, shoved it in her jacket pocket and brushed her fingers through her hair.

Connie tucked the coat under her arm and handed back the cup and bar. "I'll hang this on the back of a chair."

That must be what Hank meant about fussing. "Thanks."

She led Zoe to an empty chair. "Sit. You can drink your coffee and eat your candy bar. I have a feeling we're going to be here for a while."

Time dragged. New patients arrived. Others left. Jake checked on Denali. Hank kept bugging the nurses for news, but could get none.

More of Sean's friends and family members arrived. One of them, Jake's pregnant wife, Carly, brought a container of chocolate chip cookies. Zoe ate one, but only to be polite. Her appetite seemed to have disappeared even though she hadn't eaten lunch.

She looked around at the crowd that had gathered. On Thanksgiving, no less.

If friends were the measure of the man, not many could match Sean Hughes. Her instincts about him had been right. Zoe had never met nicer, more generous people in her life. Talk about being there for someone in good times or in bad.

She longed for the same kind of connection with her family and friends. But her family was too busy and her friends were more interested in partying and shopping. The realization left her feeling a little hollow.

The tension in the waiting room kept rising while they

waited for more information. Connie shredded her tissue. Zoe got her another one as well as a home magazine for Connie to read.

"Want to see if there are any good recipes or decorating ideas for Christmas in here with me?" Zoe asked.

"I'd love to," Connie said.

Together they pored over the articles and pictures, but the distraction only went so far. Each time the doors leading to and from the emergency department opened, everyone stared. They wanted—needed—to hear more about Sean's condition.

"Would you like me to talk to the nurse?" Zoe offered.

"Thanks, but let Hank keep trying," Connie said. "He's not one for sitting still long. Besides, I'd rather keep you to myself."

Her words made Zoe feel good inside. Accepted. She really liked Sean's family and all his friends. She would have felt better, however, if they knew the truth.

A man dressed in surgical scrubs walked out of the two double doors leading to the emergency department. Silence fell over the waiting area. Several people stood.

"Mr. and Mrs. Hughes," the doctor said.

Hank stepped forward. Connie rose. She reached a hand for Zoe, clutching her forearm and dragging her forward with her.

Zoe didn't belong with them, but she could not deny that desperate grip on her arm. She held her breath, hoping for the best.

"Whatever you have to say to us, the others can hear," Hank said, a slight tremor to his voice. "We're all family here."

"I'm Dr. Erickson," the man said. "Sean's head CT is negative for a serious injury. No skull fracture or internal bleeding, but he has suffered a closed head injury. A concussion. Sean is being admitted by the trauma surgeon."

Hank opened and closed his mouth several times.

"But you said it wasn't serious," Zoe said. As soon as the

words were out of her mouth, she realized she never should have spoken.

"The concussion is mild." Dr. Erickson's eyes darkened. "I'm more concerned about his left leg. Sean has a tib-fib fracture. Tibia and fibula. It's an open fracture so he's being given Ancef, an antibiotic."

"A broken leg can't be that bad," Connie said.

Hank put his arm around her.

"Certainly not life threatening," the doctor agreed with a tired smile. "But he will need surgery tonight. An orthopedist will use a plate and screws. It's called ORIF. That means open reduction, internal fixation. Basically the fracture is closed and the fracture immobilized or fixed with hardware."

The more the doctor said, the tighter Connie held on to Zoe.

Zoe wished she could ease some of the worry. This wasn't her place, but she wanted to help Connie. "Isn't this a pretty common procedure?"

"Yes," he said. "This method has been used often and quite successfully."

Connie sighed and loosened her grip slightly.

"Sean also has an ankle sprain on the contralateral side."

Zoe blinked. "The what?"

"He sprained his right ankle," Dr. Erickson explained. "If you'll come with me, you can see him now."

Sean's parents followed the doctor. Connie still had hold of Zoe and pulled her with them.

Her snowboarding boots felt as if they were filled with cement. Zoe had already said enough. Too much really. "I'll stay here. Sean will want to see you."

Connie didn't release her.

Hank smiled. "I'm sure he'd rather see your pretty face."

Zoe let herself be dragged forward.

She wanted to see Sean, but he had a concussion. What if he didn't recognize her?

It was just a mild concussion, but still…head injuries could make people forget things. She remembered the professional football player—a quarterback—she'd dated a couple of times. He'd gotten concussions being sacked on the field and had some memory issues.

What if Sean didn't remember she was supposed to be his girlfriend? What if he didn't remember her at all?

Her insides quivered.

Okay, the odds of that were slim, but with her string of bad luck anything was possible. Zoe's heart pounded so hard she thought it might burst out of her chest.

That would be such a cruel way for his parents to discover the truth. These nice people didn't deserve that. If only she'd had the guts to tell the truth when she arrived, but she hadn't. She didn't mind paying that price, but she minded if the Hughes did.

Maybe if Zoe stood in the back, far away from the bed and kept her mouth shut or rather said as little as possible, Sean wouldn't even notice her. Maybe…

Sean felt as if he were floating. He felt a pressure in his left leg and in his head. Far-off pain like the distant rumble of thunder. Threatening, but nothing like the lightning jabs that had seared him earlier.

Beeps, machines. Footsteps sounded.

He was in a hospital in a large room with surgical lights. He had been stripped naked. A huge number of people had evaluated him, a posse of medical professionals, but it was quiet now. Someone had covered him with a gown. Another had laid a warm blanket across his chest.

That was what he knew about his situation.

But he was too out of it to care.

He probably should care, but all he wanted to do was drift off on the cloud of whatever medication they'd pumped into him.

"Oh, honey."

The sound of his mother's voice forced Sean to open his eyes. The light blinded him. He blinked. It didn't help. He closed his eyelids, thankful for the darkness once again. "Mom."

His voice sounded different. Husky. Disembodied, almost.

She kissed his cheek. "Thank goodness you're in one piece."

Was he in one piece? He didn't feel all here. Everything seemed fuzzy. His left leg was immobilized. His right ankle had been elevated.

Sleep. He wanted to sleep.

"That had to have been some fall, son," his dad said. "I hope the mountain is as beat up as you are."

"I…" Sean forced himself awake. "I don't remember."

He'd been riding down on his board. Something had snapped, and he'd felt as if he were flying. Someone—Sean couldn't remember who—had mentioned a broken binding, but he hadn't a clue what actually happened out there except… he hadn't been alone.

Panic bolted through him. His chest tightened.

He tried to sit up, but couldn't. The dull ache in his head sharpened to a knife's edge.

"Denali?" he croaked.

No one said anything. He thought he heard his mom tell someone to speak.

"Denali?" Sean repeated, firmer this time, even though it hurt.

"Denali's fine," an unfamiliar feminine voice said. "She's in your truck in the hospital parking lot."

The woman's words brought instant relief.

He cracked open his eyes, straining to see her, but couldn't see past the lights and equipment. They'd connected some annoying monitor to him that beeped at regular intervals.

"Jake told me she stayed with you and kept you warm until help arrived," the woman added.

"She's my good girl." The medication took the edge off the pain in his head. Denali was fine. Now he could sleep.

"She's a very good girl," the mystery woman agreed.

He'd heard that voice before. Somewhere.

"Are you in a lot of pain?" Connie asked.

Sean wiggled his right hand where they had inserted an IV for medication. "Whatever they're giving me makes me not care so much about the pain."

"You'll be headed to surgery shortly, Sean," the doctor said. "An open fracture needs immediate attention. A good thing your tetanus vaccination is up to date or you would have needed a shot on top of everything else."

"He never liked shots," Connie said.

Sean should let it go, but couldn't. "I was a kid, Mom."

"You're still my kid, Sean."

He wasn't about to argue that would make him a thirty-three-year-old kid.

"You'll meet the orthopedic surgeon in pre-op holding," the doctor said.

Sean struggled to focus. "How bad is it, Doc?"

"You took quite a fall, but with time and rehabilitation you shouldn't have any permanent damage. You'll be able to snowboard and climb again," the doctor explained. "You're a lucky man, Sean."

"Lucky," he repeated with his eyes still closed. He was happy to be alive, but he wondered when he could get started on rehab, when he would be able to climb and board again. He needed to get back up the mountain.

Thinking hurt. He squeezed his eyes shut more.

"The lights seem a little bright in here," the woman who Sean couldn't quite place said. "Is it okay if I turn them down, Doctor?"

"Go ahead," the doctor said. "Try opening your eyes now."

Sean opened his eyes slowly. The lights had been dimmed. Better, but he still felt as if his brain were stuffed with cotton. He looked around the room. The doctor in scrubs. His mom in her trademark pilgrim apron. His dad with his hands shoved in his pockets. Monitoring equipment with blinking lights and digital numbers. A pair of female breasts.

Sean blinked. The breasts were still there. High, perky, round.

At least his eyesight hadn't been affected by the head injury. Maybe this wasn't a hospital, but heaven. A heaven full of female breasts sounded about perfect to him.

"See, Zoe." Connie sounded less worried. "It's a good thing you came with us. You made him smile."

"And sent his pulse rate up, too," Hank added.

Zoe. Sean knew that name. He looked up from her chest to find a brown-haired woman staring at him from behind some sort of medical equipment. The angel breasts matched an angelic face. Young. Cute. Concerned. "Zoe?"

Maybe he'd rattled his brain even more than he thought. He had no idea who she was, but she sure was easy on his eyes.

"Don't you worry, honey," Connie said to him. "I had Jake drive her down in your truck. We're all taking really good care of your Zoe."

Your Zoe.

His Zoe.

Zoe.

It all came back to him in a harsh, painful rush.

That face, pink-cheeked, peering up at him from the side of the road with her snowboard and pack at her feet. He'd offered her a…ride, he remembered. A ride and turkey dinner at his parents' house. But there was more…. He searched his hazy brain. His grandmother's ring in the safe-deposit box at the bank. His girlfriend meeting the family for the first time.

Oh, hell.

His girlfriend.

"Zoe," he repeated, this time with a hint of urgency. "You okay?"

"Yes." She approached the bed tentatively and touched his left hand gently. Her skin felt warm, the pads of her fingers soft against his skin. "I'm so sorry about all of this."

She wasn't only talking about his fall. He squeezed her hand. "More than you bargained for."

"It's okay." Her eyes clouded. "Are you...all right with this?"

He glanced at his parents who were watching them with satisfied looks on their faces. She really was a trooper for continuing the charade. "Fine."

"You should rest." She glanced at his parents. "Get better."

"Yeah."

She wet her lips. "Is there anything you need?"

Actually he could think of something that would make this crappy day a little better.

Sean stared at her mouth, at her full, glossed lips. Yes, he knew exactly what he needed to see him through surgery and recovery. She was his "girlfriend" after all. "Come closer."

Zoe leaned over him. Strands of her below-the-shoulder brown hair swung forward.

He raised his hand to touch her hair. Brown. Silky. "Nice," he whispered.

She smiled at him, her cheeks flushed.

Sean knew Zoe was trapped. Still, he couldn't resist taking advantage of the situation to steal a kiss. He could blame it later on his head injury or the pain medication, but he was going to kiss her if it was the last thing he did.

He reached up and drew her head toward him.

Surprise filled her eyes. Her mouth parted, but she said nothing.

With an extreme amount of effort, he raised his head slightly off the pillow and kissed her on the lips. She tasted like chocolate and when she kissed him back something else. Heaven. The way he felt standing on a summit.

The surprising realization jolted him. He felt as if he'd hit his head again. Sean rested his head on the pillow. He closed his eyes with a smile on his face for what he'd gotten away with and for her kissing him back. He kept hold of Zoe's hand, as much for his sake as his parents'.

"After his surgery he'll be taken to a room upstairs."

The doctor's voice cut through the darkness in Sean's brain. "There's a surgical waiting area for family members."

"We'll wait there," Connie said. "Right, Zoe?"

"Yes," she said to Sean's relief. "What about Denali…?"

Zoe truly was an angel to think of his dog.

"Jake can take her to Hannah's," Sean muttered.

"Hannah and Garrett Willingham have dogsat for Sean before," Connie explained to Zoe. "They won't mind, and their kids will love having Denali around."

"That settles it, then," Zoe said.

"This isn't the Thanksgiving you expected, Zoe," Connie said.

"I don't think this was the Thanksgiving any of us expected, but that doesn't matter," Zoe replied. "We all have something to be very thankful for today."

Sean couldn't imagine what she was talking about. He forced open his eyes once again. "What's that?"

Her tender gaze met his. "You're going to be okay."

The warmth of her words wrapped around his heart the way they had earlier. Only this time it didn't feel as uncomfortable.

He was going to be okay.

A part of him just wished she would hang around until he was better. He kind of liked having her pretend to be his girlfriend.

CHAPTER THREE

THE AROMA of Thanksgiving dinner filled the air, making the atrium lobby area smell more like a restaurant than a hospital. Nurses had rolled in a cart to hold the dinner delivered by Sean's cousin, Mary Sue Townsend, wife of the sheriff's deputy.

Zoe sat at a round table with Sean's parents. All three were eager for an update on the ongoing surgery, but so far no word. She poked at the food on her paper plate with a plastic fork.

"Please eat something, Zoe," Connie encouraged. "I know you're worried, but Sean wouldn't want you to go hungry."

Zoe stared down at her rapidly congealing gravy. She appreciated the dinner and the thought behind it even more. Slices of turkey jostled with stuffing and mashed potatoes. Homemade cranberry sauce ran into the green-bean casserole. It smelled delicious, but her appetite was gone.

All she could think about was…Sean.

How was the surgery on his leg going?

Why had he kissed her?

And why did her lips still tingle from his kiss?

"It could be a long night," Hank added. "You'll need your strength."

The concern in his voice made Zoe take a bite of stuffing. Warm, but a little soggy.

"That wasn't so bad, was it?" Connie asked.

"Delicious." The satisfied smiles on Hank's and Connie's faces made Zoe ignore the lump in her stomach. She would eat whether she wanted to or not. They had enough on their minds. She didn't want to add to their real worries for their son.

She forced the moist stuffing down her dry throat.

Connie exchanged a relieved glance with Hank.

Zoe sipped from her bottle of lemon-lime soda. The cool liquid quenched her thirst, but did little to calm her churning stomach. Her tummy had felt all fluttery since the touch of Sean's lips against hers.

What was going on?

She had kissed a lot of guys over the years. More than her mother would want her to admit. More than Zoe could even remember.

Yet Sean's kiss disturbed her. As much as she would like to dismiss it as a combination of his pain medications and a show for his parents, the glint in Sean's eyes right before he kissed her, and the way he kissed her, clearly wasn't an innocent gesture. Zoe had been surprised at the heat considering he was banged up and hurting. She'd also been shocked by her reaction.

Sean's kiss had shot straight to Zoe's heart, leaving her bothered and confused. The way he'd flirted with her in the truck had been fun, but the way he invited her to dinner and up the mountain with him had made her feel special. Very special.

She wanted to kiss him again.

Stupid, stupid Zoe.

She shoved a piece of turkey with some gravy into her mouth as if food could make this better.

Allowing a second kiss to occur would be beyond dumb and totally irresponsible. Her mother was right. Zoe was too impulsive. She hadn't always acted responsibly, especially in matters of the heart. More than once, she'd been taken advantage of, and even lied to.

The stakes were too high to allow herself to be taken in again. No more plunging headfirst and heart first into relationships. Her heart had to remain immune to kisses, to handsome men, to…everything.

Including Sean Hughes.

Zoe liked him more than she should for knowing him for so short a time. As great as Sean seemed, she couldn't trust herself not to mess things up somehow.

She ate her dinner roll.

"Do you want another roll?" Connie asked.

"No, thank you," Zoe said. "But all the food is delicious."

"We'll have to see about having a makeup Thanksgiving dinner once Sean is out of the hospital." Connie picked up her iced tea. "A welcome-home-get-well celebration."

"I'm sure he'll appreciate that." Zoe tried a bite of the homemade cranberry sauce. It tasted bittersweet.

She wanted to help Sean out, but at what risk? Her own feelings? Her heart?

If her mother found out what she was up to, Zoe would lose access to her trust fund. And for what? A cute guy, who offered a ride up the mountain, invited her to dinner with his family and kissed her so tenderly and with such emotion she couldn't think straight?

Zoe slumped in her chair.

Somehow she forced herself to continue to eat. She ate a slice of pumpkin pie topped with whipped cream, but she barely tasted one of her all-time favorite desserts. All Zoe could think about was the smile on Sean's face and the gleam in his eye when he was telling her about the really good pie on their drive up to Timberline. If only she hadn't told him to go on when he said he'd board with her at the resort…

Once dinner was finished, they made their way to the surgical waiting room. The tension seemed to escalate. She glanced at the clock on the wall, mindful of the time since they'd wheeled him away. She wasn't the only one. The clock became everyone's prime focus. Zoe could almost feel each minute tick by.

She hated waiting. It reminded her too much of her experience with her dad.

Goose bumps prickled her skin.

No, she told herself. Sean was going to be okay. The doctor
had said so.

Connie paced. "It's taking a long time."

"He had to go to pre-op first. Then there's the anesthesiolo-
gist. I'd imagine putting in a plate and screws takes a little
time," Zoe said, as much for her own benefit as Connie's.

Hank nodded. "Better they go slow and get it right, than
have them rush and need to go back in."

The words didn't stop Connie from pacing.

"You're going to wear yourself out," Hank said finally.

"I hope so." Connie's voice sounded tired, strained. "Sleep
would be better than worrying."

Half an hour later, the orthopedic surgeon, Dr. Vandenhoff,
entered the waiting area. He wore sweat-stained green surgical
scrubs.

Connie clutched Hank.

"The surgery went well," Dr. Vandenhoff said. "We washed
out debris from the fracture. Inserted the plate and screws.
Sean is in recovery."

Connie sighed. "Thank goodness."

"Thank you, Doctor," Hank said.

Relief welled up inside of Zoe. Tears stung the corner of
her eyes. "Yes, thank you."

She was thankful, because the sooner Sean was feeling
better, the sooner she could leave.

The sooner she would be safe.

Sean felt as if a white-noise machine had replaced his brain.
He had no idea how long he'd been asleep or what had oc-
curred while he was sleeping. The familiar pressure in his
head and legs remained, as did the far-off ache.

Pain.

You're a very lucky man, Sean.

Yeah, right. He wondered if that was what the doctor said to everyone who passed through the E.R.

A loud snore ripped through the air. Sean forced open his heavy eyelids.

The lights in the hospital room had been dimmed, but he could make out a sleeping figure in a chair. Another deep, familiar snore sounded.

His dad.

Sean grinned and winced at the same time. It was great his dad was here, but man, the snoring sounded like his chain saw.

Sean noticed something different in this room—the smell. The scent of flowers masked the typical, sterile hospital scent.

"You're awake," a woman said.

He struggled to place the voice, fighting the fog inside his head. Not just a woman, he realized, pleased. Zoe.

His Zoe.

"Would you like some water?" she asked.

He felt as if he'd swallowed a bag of cotton balls or his throat had been scoured with sandpaper. "Please."

A straw sticking out from the lid of a plastic cup poked at his lips. "The nurse said you should take little sips," Zoe cautioned.

Sean fought to raise his head. He didn't care what the nurse had said. She didn't know how thirsty he was. He sucked the water, choked and coughed. Somehow he managed not to spit it out. He cleared his throat. "Nurse was right."

Zoe supported the back of his neck with one hand, handed him a tissue with another and eased him back onto his pillow. "That's what you said before."

Before. He didn't remember.

Sean focused on Zoe standing next to the bed. Her clear, blue eyes looked at him with such compassion his breath caught in his throat. Her long-sleeved T-shirt fit tight across her chest and raised his temperature ten degrees. Her jeans clung to her hips, showing him he'd been right about the curves hidden beneath her snowboarding jacket.

He smiled. "You're still here."

Which made him feel unexpectedly relieved.

She glanced over at his dad and back at Sean with an uncertain smile. "Where else would your girlfriend be?"

"In bed. With me." He tried to wink, but wasn't sure he managed one. Right now he couldn't manage much of anything.

She shook her head, her smile growing. "There isn't room."

Not to mention he couldn't fool around with her. But the idea of her curled warm against his side was surprisingly appealing.

"I don't mind being cramped," he said.

"I might hurt you."

"Promise?"

She laughed. "Okay, you're feeling better."

"I'm not feeling much at all."

Zoe patted his hand lightly. Her touch soothed and comforted him. "That's probably a very good thing right now."

"I'll be fine."

"I'm sure you will."

"What about you?" he asked.

She glanced at his dad once again. "I'm fine, too."

Fine, huh? Zoe looked tired. Sean didn't like that. "What time is it?"

"Four o'clock."

"In the morning?" he asked.

"The afternoon."

Sean noticed gray light streaking through the window. A mylar balloon floated from a red string and two bright floral arrangements sat on the counter. He remembered none of those things. He must have been out of it awhile.

"Where did you sleep last night?" he asked.

She looked down at the IV in his right arm. "Here."

He looked at his dad asleep on the recliner. "Where's my mom?"

"At a nearby motel," Zoe explained. "Your mom's been through a lot in the last twenty-four hours. She needs to rest and relax away from the hospital for a little while."

"You're giving her a break."

Zoe rubbed the small of her back. "Your dad is here, too."

As if on cue, his father let loose another snore.

"My dad's working real hard."

The corners of Zoe's mouth curved.

In spite of her smile, she had to be tired sitting and sleeping upright. This was going above and beyond the call of phony girlfriend duty. Sean couldn't let it continue. "I can come clean to my folks about us."

"And your family and friends, too?"

Sean had forgotten about them. He tried to think of how to handle this. It wasn't easy. "Breaking up might be easier than trying to explain things." Although the fallout over his supposed breakup with a girl his family obviously approved of could be worse than their comments about settling down. That wouldn't make for a very nice Christmas. "Actually there might be less drama if I tell the truth."

"Whatever you think best."

Best would be her body next to his. He'd settle for another kiss. His father stirred awake.

"I'll explain everything to them once I'm out of the hospital," Sean said.

"That's fine."

"You'll stay?" he asked, knowing the answer he wanted to hear.

Uncertainty filled her eyes.

"Until I'm out of here. The hospital," he clarified.

Time seemed to slow while he waited for her answer.

Say yes.

"Until you're out of the hospital," Zoe said.

Sean smiled. That was good enough for him.

* * *

Zoe couldn't remember what day it was. She stared at her exhausted eyes and pale skin in the mirror of the women's restroom. She looked as if she'd been up half the night. Which she had. Again.

Zoe yawned. She was running on fumes. Not even caffeine would help at this point. She had spent another night at the hospital while Connie and Hank slept at the motel. They'd decided to split into shifts. Zoe had offered to take the night shift to limit her interaction with Sean's family and friends. There was only so much pretending she could take. She didn't like misleading people. The sooner everyone knew the truth the better. She didn't know how much longer she could keep up the charade.

Sean's parents were up in his room now. They had arrived minutes ago to relieve her. A tag team of family and friends would spell them throughout the day.

Zoe splashed cold water on her face. It didn't help. She couldn't wait to return to the motel. Connie had generously rented a room with two queen-size beds and handed Zoe a key so she, too, would have a place to sleep outside of the hospital.

She dried her face with a paper towel from the dispenser above the counter and tossed it into the trash. She would give the Hughes a few more minutes alone before Hank drove her to the motel. They needed time together as a family.

And Zoe needed time away from Sean.

She applied lip gloss. The rest of her makeup as well as her backpack were at the motel.

She liked Sean. He wasn't just a pretty face with a hot body. His injuries hadn't dampened his sense of humor. He hadn't complained or seemed all that down. In fact, he'd been handling his situation with a courage and attitude she respected.

Too bad respect wasn't the only thing she felt for him.

The way Sean looked at her when he woke up from one of his naps made her feel special even in the middle of the night. He wanted her at his side. She wanted to be there for him. Feeling wanted was a whole lot better than feeling like a screwup.

For once she was no longer oopsie-baby, the nickname given to her by her older brothers, or Zany Zoe, which her friends had called her after all her trouble with the tabloids. She preferred being simply Zoe.

Zoe Flynn, she reminded herself. Zoe Carrington had all but ceased to exist the past few weeks. Maybe that wasn't such a bad thing.

The more time she spent with Sean, his family and friends, the more she liked them and the less she missed her old life. She could never imagine Connie or Hank sending one of their kids away so they would learn responsibility and wouldn't cause any problems. Zoe wished the Hughes were her family and she'd be spending Christmas with them, not alone in a strange town somewhere far away from home.

She felt a pang in her heart.

Stop. Now.

Thinking like that was too dangerous. And not possible. December twenty-fifth was too far away.

Sean was handling his pain better. He'd been visited by a physical therapist and an occupational therapist. He would be out of here before Zoe knew it, and so would she.

She wasn't his real girlfriend. He didn't really need her. Nor did Connie and Hank or any of the other family members or friends Zoe had met.

The realization made her heart drop to her feet with a resounding splat. She was all alone and had to remain that way until after the special election.

Feeling sad and even more tired, she returned to Sean's room. He had fallen asleep again.

She glanced around.

Crayon drawings by the children of his extended family and friends hung on the walls. One was a picture of Denali. Another was a mountain surrounded by space ships. More flowers and balloon bouquets had been delivered along with cards. A part of her wished she could send Sean one of the lovely flower arrangements, but all she could afford at the moment was a single rosebud without the vase. Zoe sighed.

"Would you mind running down to the gift shop with Connie before I take you to the motel?" Hank asked quietly. "She wants to pick up some things for her shift."

"Not a problem," Zoe said.

"I'll stay here in case Sean wakes up," Hank added.

Downstairs in the gift shop, Connie tucked a newspaper under her arm and studied the candy selection. She had a real sweet tooth. "While you were gone, the occupational therapist stopped by. She gave her recommendations to the discharge planner."

Relief Sean was doing well enough to be discharged pulsed through Zoe. "That's wonderful news."

Good news for Sean and his family. As for her...

It was best if she moved on.

"I just hope Sean doesn't fight their recommendations," Connie said. "He can be stubborn sometimes."

"He also has a concussion, a sprained ankle and a broken leg." Zoe scanned the newspaper headlines. She hadn't watched much TV in Sean's hospital room because she hadn't wanted to disturb his sleep. She'd been too tired when she got to the motel. She felt as if she were emerging from a cocoon and needed to catch up on what she'd missed the last couple of days. "Stubborn will only take him so far."

"He may need you to tell him that."

She flashed Connie a supportive smile. "If he does, I will."

That was the least Zoe could do, even if Sean wouldn't listen to her. She owed the Hughes family big-time. They had provided a warm place for her to sleep and shower, dropped off food for her at Sean's hospital room and given her rides back and forth to the motel. She hadn't spent a dime since buying her lift ticket on Thanksgiving morning. She now had enough money to make it until her monthly allowance would be deposited into her checking account on the first of

December. She would find a way to repay their generosity somehow, someday.

Zoe glimpsed the cover of a tabloid and did a double take. She reread the words in the top corner of the front page.

Party Animal Zoe Carrington Caged?

Her heart plummeted to her feet.

She glanced at the name of the tabloid. *Weekly Secrets*.

Anger burned. They were one of the worst gossip rags out there, the first to publish the photos of her at that club with Lonzo the liar. They'd only gone on two dates, but he'd made it out to be the love affair of the century. The lying, married jerk.

She saw Connie shuffling through greeting cards. Zoe wanted to ignore the headline, but curiosity made her reach for the paper. She opened the tabloid. A file photo of her, with blond highlighted hair, a ton of makeup and an expensive designer cocktail dress, greeted her. She cringed.

Party Animal Zoe Carrington Caged!
Garrett Malloy and Fred Silvers

Political insiders claim Governor Vanessa Carrington, currently embroiled in a special election for a coveted U.S. Senate seat, has banished her youngest daughter, Zoe, from the state, possibly the country. The move is not surprising given the scandal that erupted when photos of the lovely socialite and heartthrob actor Lonzo Green surfaced two months ago.

Zoe claimed Green told her he was divorced, but he countered her statement by saying, "Young women have a tendency to hear only what they want to hear when they are in love."

When asked about his missing ex-paramour, Green replied, "No comment."

His indifference is surprising since the publicity resulting from the scandal is widely credited with Green landing a lead role in the highly anticipated blockbuster *Tsunami*. No doubt he hopes to ride the wave straight to the A-list. As for Green's wife, soap opera actress Britt Bayer, she has been at his side ever since the story of her husband's torrid affair broke.

Sources close to the governor claim twenty-four-year-old Zoe simply wanted a break from her hectic social schedule. But if that's the case, why has no one seen or heard from Zoe?

"A break means a short trip to Paris or New York or Milan," gossip blogger and hanger-on Charlotte Rafferty said. "There are always parties. Appearances. Photos. Zoe constantly sent tweets until her disappearance, and her Facebook page hasn't been updated in weeks. Something has definitely happened to her, but the governor keeps shutting down any attempts at an official investigation into Zoe's whereabouts."

There is speculation the governor may have committed her wild child to a mental health or rehab facility to avoid more embarrassing headlines that would compromise her senate run.

If you know the whereabouts of Zoe Carrington, please contact us here at *Weekly Secrets*. She's one of our favorite headline makers, and we'd like to make sure she's safe.

Safe. Yeah, right. Zoe grimaced. The only thing tabloids cared about was selling more papers. She only interested them when she was doing something scandalous or glamorous. Nothing else rated with them.

She glanced at Connie who still stood at the card display.

Disgusted to be touching such trash, Zoe shoved the piece of garbage back into its slot on the rack. If they were looking for her, others would be, too. Not good.

Okay, she no longer had blond hair and wasn't wearing much makeup now. She barely recognized herself, but that didn't mean someone else might not put two and two together.

The longer Zoe stayed in a city the size of Portland, the better the chance of being discovered. She needed to find a place to hide away. A small, cheap town with an ATM where she could access her checking account.

A cell phone rang. Connie's.

One of the many family members calling or something about Sean? Zoe's muscles bunched.

Connie answered the phone before the second ring with a strained hello, but soon her eyes lit up and she smiled.

Thank goodness. Zoe relaxed.

"That's great, Hank," Connie answered, animated. "Yes, he must be feeling more like his old self. No, we'll be right up."

Zoe waited until Sean's mom had hung up. "Are they discharging him?"

"Not yet, but the press is on their way to Sean's room to interview him about his experience. A rescuer being rescued by his own unit." Connie set three candy bars, a get-well card and a newspaper on the counter. She pulled out her wallet. "We need to get up there."

The air rushed from Zoe's lungs. Every single nerve ending went on alert. Being in the same building as the media was bad enough. No way could she risk being in the same room. "I'm too tired."

"Sean will want you there."

No, he wouldn't. Especially if he knew the truth about her. Zoe forced a smile. "I'm not the story. He is."

Connie didn't look convinced as she paid the elderly cashier wearing a pink jacket.

Zoe would try another tack. "There's going to be a lot happening up there, and the room's not that big. I'm going to stop by the cafeteria for a coffee. Maybe I'll make it back before they're finished."

Emphasis on *maybe*.

"Okay." Connie picked up her bag of purchases from the counter. "But if Sean asks—"

"I'll tell him you wanted me up there," Zoe interrupted. "You'd better hurry so you don't miss anything."

"You're sure?"

"Yes." Zoe had never been more certain of anything in her life. "Now go."

The camera crews were gone. The last reporter had left.

Where was Zoe?

Sean felt cranky and deflated.

The news from his discharge planner wasn't making him feel any better. He was used to taking care of other people, not needing someone to take care of him.

"I'm sorry, Sean." Meghan, a well-dressed thirtysomething woman with bright red hair piled on top of her head, spoke gently, as if her soft voice would ease his frustration. "An independent discharge is not possible. You cannot ambulate safely with both your fracture and a sprained ankle."

"I understand the OT's assessment." He was still on pain medication, but not even that was going to make him go along with this nonsense. "But really, I'm used to living alone. I can take care of myself. My ankle will be fine. I'll hire a physical therapist to help me with the recommended exercises. I have friends to help with my dog. It won't be a problem."

Zoe entered the room quietly. Relief washed over him. Now he might have an ally and—

"Problem or not, you're going to be using a walker for the first couple of weeks," Meghan said. "You'll need help preparing meals and bathing. Living alone in your current condition is not possible."

"You don't know me."

Connie opened her mouth. Hank tapped her thigh. His mother pressed her lips together.

"I don't," Meghan said patiently. "But I'm required to follow what OT recommends. A recommendation your orthopedic surgeon agrees with."

Sean gritted his teeth.

Zoe walked toward his bed. "What are Sean's options?"

"The first is a sniff," Meghan said.

"A what?" Connie asked.

"Skilled nursing facility, also known as a SNF," Meghan explained. "Hiring homecare is another option. But usually the best solution, especially with a head injury, is for Sean to go home with someone capable of caring for him."

"He can stay with us," Connie said without a moment of hesitation.

Hank nodded. "That's the best option for our son."

Sean forced himself not to grimace. He didn't want to hurt his parents' feelings. "Mom. Dad. I appreciate the offer, but I'm a little old to move back home."

His mom glanced at his dad. The determined look in her eyes told Sean she wouldn't change her mind without a fight.

He had friends and family who would gladly stay with him, but Sean didn't want to put anyone out.

"Would you mind if we discussed this in private, Meghan?" Hank asked.

"Take your time." The woman rose. "I'll be at the nurses' station."

"Thank you," Connie said.

"Would you like me to leave?" Zoe asked.

"Stay," Sean said.

"Of course you should stay," Hank said.

Connie nodded.

Silence descended on the room. Meghan closed the door behind her.

"I know you're independent, Sean, but you won't be at home with us forever." Connie spoke as if the decision had already been made. Not good. "Only until you're back on your feet and can take care of yourself."

"I can take care of myself now," Sean countered. "I can order takeout when I'm hungry. I've been on climbing trips where I haven't been able to shower."

Hank shook his head. "Your mother's right, son. Coming home with us is your best option."

Only option was what his dad meant.

Sean had to be careful here. He'd put his parents through enough these past few days. "December is a busy time of the year for both of you. I don't want you to have to take care of me on top of everything else you do at Christmastime."

"You're our son. Caring for you is not a burden." Connie's chin jutted forward. "We aren't about to let a stranger take care of you."

Sean's gaze locked with Zoe's, pleaded with her to help him out.

As if reading his mind, she walked to the side of his bed and patted his hand, the way she'd done many times before. Despite his frustration, despite the fact that she probably made the gesture to fool his parents, Sean was oddly comforted. Reassured. He spread his fingers so hers fell between his.

She smiled at him.

He smiled back.

"Unless…" Connie's voice faded.

Sean's gaze narrowed. He was willing to consider any alternative to going home with his parents. "What?"

"Zoe," she said.

"Zoe?" Sean repeated, confused.

"Me?" Zoe sounded puzzled.

"Great idea," Hank approved.

"It took me a minute to understand why you didn't want to come home with us, but I finally figured it out," Connie said with a pleased smile. "You want your pretty girlfriend to take care of you while you recover. Not your mother. And honey, I'm perfectly fine with that."

CHAPTER FOUR

Take care of Sean?

Panic ricocheted through Zoe.

Connie might think that was a good idea, but Zoe didn't. Sure, she felt good helping the Hughes family. But she needed to say goodbye to them, not entangle herself deeper in their lives. Time to get out of here, except...

With Sean holding tightly on to her hand she wasn't going anywhere.

"I don't know how much time you've spent in Hood Hamlet, but everyone will pitch in and help with Sean's recovery," Hank said to her. "You won't find a more supportive community."

"The way Sean's friends have rallied around him since his accident makes it seem like a very friendly place," Zoe admitted.

"Nothing beats living near family," Connie piped in.

Hank nodded. "I wouldn't want to live anywhere else."

Sean smiled at Zoe. "It's friendly, definitely. Your typical small town. I gave living in Portland a try once, but I prefer the mountains."

The Hood Hamlet Chamber of Commerce would be proud of the Hughes for championing the town. Too bad their sales tactics were wasted on her.

"Who knows, Zoe?" Connie grinned. "You might just fall in love."

Love? The air whooshed from Zoe's lungs.

Sean's lips thinned. "Mom."

"What?" Connie feigned innocence. "Zoe might fall in love with Hood Hamlet. It's a very nice place to live."

Maybe for them, but not Zoe. She was used to city living. On her own. Not caring for someone who needed more help than she knew how to give.

Her shoulders sagged, a combination of exhaustion and frustration. They spoke as if this were a done deal, as if she would be staying in Hood Hamlet. "About taking care of Sean…"

"Yes," he said. "About that…"

"My son isn't the best patient." Connie smiled at Zoe, as if sharing a family secret. "I remember when he had chicken pox. You would have thought his world was ending."

"I was nine." Sean's chin jutted out. "Two feet of fresh powder to ride, and I was stuck in bed."

"I'm sure he'll behave better with you," Connie said.

Whether he behaved or not didn't matter. Zoe started to tell them this was a really bad idea, but stopped herself.

What could she say without giving everything away?

She would have to wait for Sean to say something, to tell them why she shouldn't be the one to take care of him.

Zoe waited. The seconds on the clock seemed to tick as slow as minutes.

Please, Sean.

Her gaze bounced between him and his parents.

What was taking him so long?

There was no point—no need—to drag out the charade any longer. He was clearly recovering. With the worst of his parents' worries allayed, it was time for Sean to tell them the truth about Zoe and his nonrelationship.

But how?

That question made her realize why Sean was hesitating. He must be trying to figure out what to say to his parents and how to explain all of this to them.

A mix of emotion churned inside Zoe. Relief at not having to continue the lie. Regret at the thought of hurting the people she'd come to care about these past few days. But in her heart, Zoe knew this needed to be done, now, no matter what the fallout.

Connie and Hank didn't want a stranger looking after their son. Well, Zoe was a stranger. Even though she liked feeling needed by his family and by Sean, she was the last person they would want to care for him.

She looked at Sean.

He lay covered with a blanket in the hospital bed, so different from the man she'd met a few days ago on the side of the road. Stubble covered his face. A cut near his chin had scabbed over. The dark bruise on his cheek was fading. His hair was sticking up all over the place.

Oh, he was still handsome. A few cuts and purple blotches didn't change his amazing bone structure and his warm, hazel-green eyes. But his physical weakness, his vulnerability struck at her heart and her insecurities.

Zoe's chest ached.

Sean needed someone who knew what they were doing, someone who could make sure he had everything he needed while recovering.

That wasn't her. She had the necessary skills to be his personal shopper, not his caretaker.

Besides, no matter how vulnerable Sean Hughes might look at the moment, he wasn't a man to play doctor or house with. She shouldn't play with him period.

She was vulnerable, too.

Careful and cautious, remember?

Zoe toyed with the edge of his blanket with her free hand. "Sean…"

His gaze met hers.

Something passed between them. She chewed on the inside of her cheek. They were in this little ruse together, but it had morphed into something neither had imagined.

He squeezed her hand. "Mom, Dad, would you mind giving me and Zoe a few minutes alone?"

Connie jumped to her feet. "Of course."

"We'll wait outside," Hank added.

Sean's parents exited the room. As soon as the door latched, he grimaced. "I'm sorry about all this."

"We have to tell them the truth."

"I know," he agreed. "You must have some place else you need to be."

Zoe had no set itinerary, simply a list of places she couldn't go: home, Los Angeles, New York, London and Paris. "Not really, but that's beside the point."

"Your family and your boyfriend must be expecting you home at some point."

"Traveling was actually my mother's idea. My brothers are older than me. We're not very close. I'm actually estranged from my family right now," Zoe admitted. "And I don't have a boyfriend. A real one, that is."

"Where do you live?"

She thought about the apartment in Los Angeles she'd been forced to give up before setting off on her own. "I don't have a permanent address at the moment."

He studied her with an unreadable expression on his face. "What about a job?"

"I'm between jobs."

His eyes locked on hers.

She knew exactly what he was thinking. "No way."

"Why not?" he asked.

"We're not in a relationship." She kept her voice low in case Hank and Connie walked back in. "We're strangers."

"We're past the point of being strangers, Zoe."

"Your family and friends have been so nice to me," she said. "They've made me feel welcomed and accepted. I don't like lying to them."

"You've helped them get through this, Zoe. Me, too. We all appreciate that."

She liked feeling useful, but she had her trust fund, her future to consider. "If they knew the truth…"

"They'll never have to know."

"I can't stay here forever."

"I'll take care of it."

"That's what you said before."

He smiled, as if a charming grin could make everything better. "I haven't left the hospital yet."

Okay, his smile did help. A little. But she needed to be smart about this. She hadn't been smart about so many other things in her life. "It's too complicated. I haven't dealt well with complications in the past."

"You're selling yourself short."

"I'm not. If you knew…"

"I know this is a better deal for me than you," Sean admitted. "I'm willing to do whatever it takes. You'll be paid a salary. You'll also get room and board."

She didn't know whether to be insulted or reassured. "You want to pay me to take care of you?"

"Yes," he said. "I'd have to pay for home health care."

"Insurance would cover that."

"I'd rather have you there." He squeezed her hand again.

Zoe's heart bumped. That only added to her rising doubts. "I don't know."

"There are easier ways to earn money," he said. "You heard my mom. I'm not a good patient. But I'll try to be better."

Zoe could try, too. She could—

No, wait.

She should forget about this. Going along with Sean's proposal wasn't a smart idea. She should say no and walk away, yet curiosity wouldn't let her.

"What would I have to do exactly? If I took the job," she qualified.

He eyes brightened at her apparent weakening. "Walk Denali. Pretend to be madly in love with me in front of my parents. Drive me to work and appointments. Wait on me hand and foot."

A couple of those didn't sound too difficult.

In fact, the job sounded perfect given her need to stay out of the spotlight for the duration of her mother's campaign. A small town like Hood Hamlet might be the perfect place to hide. If she could live off her salary, her mother would see she had learned to manage her money. This sounded almost too good to be true. And in Zoe's experience, that meant trouble.

She'd learned nothing was ever as good as it sounded, but that hadn't kept her from hoping, wishing, it would be. All she ever wanted was to be accepted for who she was— loved—and that had often led her to ignore warning signs and even her own gut instinct. She didn't want to repeat the same pattern.

Restlessly, she moved away from the side of his bed. Zoe couldn't think when Sean was watching. She walked along the row of colorful, fragrant bouquets lined up on the windowsill. Roses, a mixed bouquet of fall-colored blossoms and Stargazer lilies. Reading the feminine names on many of the cards made her feel strange.

Not that his social life was any of her business.

"Why me?" she asked.

"My family thinks you're my girlfriend. Who else would I ask?"

"How about Chelsea or Grace or Lulu?" Zoe read the names from the cards. Reading between the lines of one of the cards seemed to indicate a close, probably intimate, relationship. The knowledge unsettled her. "Seems to me, one of them would be more than happy to help you out."

Unexpected color appeared on his cheeks. "They don't know my family. And they would have certain expectations if I asked them to help me. You won't."

"Because anything between us is pretend."

"Because we're friends," Sean said. "I don't know too many people who would go to the lengths you've gone to for a person they'd just met. I'd tie in with you any day."

"Tie in?"

"Climber term," Sean explained. "It means I'd climb with you anytime, anywhere."

The compliment made Zoe tingle all over. She felt a little breathless. "Thanks, but you helped me first."

"You've done way more for me since then."

The sincerity in his voice brought a rush of warmth flowing through her. She returned to the side of his bed.

Sean pushed a strand of hair behind her ear.

Zoe's heart stuttered. His gesture felt so intimate, so natural, so right. The impulse to agree to take care of him was so strong she pressed her lips together. She couldn't give in that easily. Sean Hughes wasn't just some guy who needed help. He was dangerous to both her senses and her hormones. And his family had already touched her heart.

"What are you thinking?" he asked.

She liked him enough, trusted him enough, to tell the truth. Or as much of it as she could.

"My mother thinks I'm too impulsive. She wants me to be more responsible."

"What could be more responsible than taking care of an injured friend?"

Not even her mother could find fault with Zoe taking care of a friend. Except that Sean's kiss on Thanksgiving before his surgery hadn't been at all friendlike. "It might cramp your style."

"Huh?"

"If we're supposed to be having a relationship, you won't be able to date."

"The same goes for you."

She shrugged. "I'm not looking for a relationship."

"That makes two of us."

She thought about his kiss, about the way he touched her. A part of her wanted to read more into his wanting her to stay. Then she remembered all the flowers from various women. "You sure about that?"

"Dating is not the same as having a relationship."

Zoe bit the inside of her cheek. "I'm not qualified."

"You've been the perfect pretend girlfriend."

"I mean I've never taken care of anyone before unless you count Popcorn, my hamster when I was nine," she explained. "He died."

"I'm going to be a lot harder to kill than a hamster."

"I don't know about that." She thought about growing up in the governor's mansion with a cook and a housekeeper. "I'm not, uh, very domestic. I feel it's fair to warn you I'm cooking and cleaning challenged."

"I don't care if you burn water," he said.

"I've never burned water, but I ruined a pan trying to heat up soup," she admitted, trying to discourage him. "I didn't know you had to add water."

"We can order takeout every night. I'll get a housecleaner to come twice a week if that makes you feel better."

"That will be expensive."

"I can afford it."

Still the cons seemed to outweigh the pros. She wished he would realize that so this would be easier. "I don't have any references."

"I don't need references," Sean said. "You've showed me the kind of person you are these past few days."

Guilt coated her mouth. He had no idea who she was. He didn't even know her real last name. Yet he was trying awfully hard to get her to stay with him.

"You're the one I want to take care of me." His earnest tone tugged at her conscience. "You're exactly what I need, Zoe."

No one had ever needed her before. Well, besides her hamster. And look how that had turned out.

Still Sean's words made Zoe feel as if she mattered, as if she wasn't as useless as people had accused her of being.

"Will you please come home with me?" he asked.

Home.

Emotion clogged her throat. If only she could go home…

But Zoe no longer knew what home meant. The place she'd grown up seemed to have drifted farther and farther away. She felt rootless, adrift, alone.

This time with the Hughes had given her a taste of both family and community. Something she hadn't really experienced since her dad died. Every day since then, Zoe's family life had been more like a job, one long PR event. That was why she'd tried to do more—to go places, see new things and bond with friends. But even then she never really felt like she was in the right place.

Was this the right place for her? The right move?

She needed to put her emotions aside and think about things logically. He was offering her a place to stay and a salary. Where else was she going to find those things without needing some sort of background check?

If she accepted Sean's offer, she could hide away in Hood Hamlet and help him out. She could show her mother she had changed, and at the same time spend Christmas with Sean's loving, accepting family.

She stared at him.

A ball of warmth settled in the center of her chest.

Christmas in Hood Hamlet with the Hughes family might help her figure out what she wanted and where she belonged. That appealed to her on multiple levels.

"Okay," Zoe said finally. "I'll do it."

Damn walker. Sean hobbled from his mother's minivan to his house. His mom had offered to drive him home while his dad took Zoe in the truck.

Sean owed a six-pack to whoever had cleared the path to his front porch this afternoon. Making his way through the snow wouldn't have been easy. It was hard enough with two bum legs and a device senior citizens used.

He glanced at his mom. She walked at a snail's pace next to him. No sense telling her to get inside before she got cold. She would only say no.

Like it or not, Connie Hughes knew what needed to be done. She'd nursed his father back from spinal surgery and her mother after a hip replacement.

"Who plowed?" Sean asked.

"Jake."

Of course, Jake Porter would make sure the path was

plowed. The guy did everything for everybody while running the Hood Hamlet Brewery, one of Sean's favorite haunts.

He glanced down at his legs and grimaced. Too bad he wouldn't be stepping in there for a pint anytime soon.

"Jake left some bottles of Twelfth Night, his new winter brew, for you in the fridge," Connie added. "But I wouldn't mix alcohol with pain medication."

Ever since the accident, people kept telling Sean what he should and shouldn't do, as if he couldn't figure things out for himself. He was a Wilderness First Responder, dammit. He had EMT training. He knew his family and friends meant well, but the constant admonitions only increased his feeling of helplessness. He wished they would keep their mouths shut. "I know, Mom."

Sean already felt off balance due to the boot on his left leg and the air cast on his right ankle. He hated feeling so fuzzy and wobbly, not knowing when a wrong step with the walker might send him flat on his ass. Falling had always been a risk when he climbed, but he'd never feared falling as much as now. He didn't want to hurt himself more.

"Sometimes pain medication can lead you to make bad decisions," she said.

Like cajoling Zoe to continue as his pretend girlfriend?

Nope, that was a good decision even though his desire to have her stick around had surprised him. He wanted to chalk it up to attraction or desperation at wanting to be home, but wasn't quite sure what compelled him. Sean had gone with his gut, and it still felt like the right move. Keeping Zoe around made him feel better. "Don't worry, Mom."

"I'm your mother," Connie said. "It's my right to worry."

Too bad, because he was worrying enough for the both of them.

Sweat beaded on Sean's forehead, even though he was wearing shorts and the temperature was in the mid-thirties. Each step took concentration, as if he were climbing in the death zone on Everest, not the front steps of his house.

He grunted. His warm breath rose on the cold air.

His mother stayed at his side, making him feel more like a four-year-old at a crowded mall than a grown man. "Sean—"

"I've got it."

With a deep breath that chilled his lungs, he managed another shaky step.

Almost inside.

"There's no rush," she said gently.

"I don't think I'll be rushing anywhere soon."

Unfortunately.

The doctor had told Sean he would need the walker before moving on to crutches. He'd laughed, thinking he could ditch the walker as soon as he arrived home. Sure he could ditch the stupid thing, but only if he wanted to crawl.

The realization was both humbling and disheartening.

He'd been an athlete his entire life and suffered his share of injuries, but nothing this serious. Now he couldn't even walk on his own.

Sean exhaled on a sigh. A lifetime of ignoring discomfort in his athletic and rescue pursuits tempered his grousing.

He was alive. He needed to concentrate on the positives.

Sean took another step. All he had to do was string a bunch of these together. No different than a steep ascent, except without using the rest step.

"You're doing great, honey," Connie encouraged, sticking close to him.

"Thanks, Mom."

Sean was glad she was here with him instead of Zoe. Maybe he would feel less wrung out by the time she arrived.

Standing on his front porch, he waited while his mom unlocked and opened the door.

He crossed the threshold and stepped onto the hardwood entry. Sean expected Denali to pounce on him, but he heard no barking, no sounds of four paws against the hardwood floor. Then he remembered. She would stay with Hannah and Garrett until Sean was steadier on his feet.

"Happy to be home?" Connie asked.

He nodded. "But I miss my girl."

"Zoe will be here soon." Connie removed her coat and hung it on the rack next to the door. She slipped off her shoes. "They were stopping by the motel to check out."

Zoe. Sean bit back a smile. He'd meant Denali, but he wouldn't mind calling Zoe his girl, too.

She might mind, however.

Sean wasn't going to do or say anything to upset Zoe. That included keeping his fantasy about her wearing a sexy nurse costume to himself. He still couldn't believe she was going to take care of him. Granted, he was paying her well, but not many people would interrupt their travel plans for a total stranger. Even fewer would pretend to be his girlfriend. He knew she'd been close to saying no. Thank goodness she hadn't. Sean hated to think how this situation would have played out without Zoe around. He would probably be settling in at his parents' house instead of his own home.

He wavered slightly and clutched the handles of the walker.

Concern clouded his mom's eyes. "You look pale."

Sean took another step. "I just need to get used to the walker."

"Take your time."

As if he had any other choice.

Slowly, molasses-in-January slowly, he made his way across the floor. The walker made a lot of noise. Maybe it was him with all the herky-jerky movement.

Finally, he reached the leather couch, turned around and sat. He settled back against the cushions. This would be his bed until he could negotiate the stairs safely. Too bad he hadn't put a bedroom on the main floor when he designed the house. At least the couch was comfortable and the television nearby.

His mother hovered over him. "Let's get that jacket off before you get too warm."

He unzipped his fleece and shrugged out of it himself.

"I appreciate the help, Mom, but my leg's broken, not my hand."

"I'll hang up your jacket and get you a glass of water." She took the coat and tucked it under her arm while she nudged the ottoman closer with her foot. "Elevate your legs."

A minute later, Sean watched her in the kitchen. She filled a glass with filtered water from the stainless-steel refrigerator, one of those French door types with the freezer on the bottom his cousin Mary Sue had suggested.

"Do you need anything else?" Connie asked.

Sean couldn't remember the last time he'd needed someone to get him a glass of water. He was coming to realize how little he could do on his own right now with his injuries and the pain medication. "No thanks, Mom."

She handed him the cup of water. "I don't mind."

But he did.

Sean took a sip and placed the glass on the end table. He heard the front door open, footsteps, voices.

Zoe.

Relief flooded him. Many women had walked into his house the same way, but none made him smile like Zoe. "Hey," he said.

"Hi." Zoe hesitated a moment before crossing the great room to stand in front of him. Leaning over, she brushed her lips over his in an awkward yet thoughtful gesture.

For his parents' sake, he realized with a stab of regret.

"How does it feel to be home?" she asked.

"Good." He cleared his dry throat. "Especially now that you're here."

Sean noticed the pleased glances exchanged by his parents. Funny thing was he wasn't pretending. He'd meant what he said.

Zoe smiled. "I'm happy to be here."

Yet he knew she wasn't as happy as he was at the moment. How could she be?

That made him feel...strange. Truth was, he needed

Zoe more than she needed him. He didn't like being in that position. Sean adjusted his legs on the ottoman.

"You need pillows," Connie said. "Zoe, dear, run and get Sean some pillows."

Zoe's startled gaze met his.

Pillows, he realized. She wouldn't know where the pillows were. She had no idea where anything was.

"Take the pillows off my bed. The blue ones," he said. Would that be enough of a hint?

"Oh, right." Gratitude filled her no longer panicked eyes. "Sorry, I'm a little tired."

"You were up all night," Hank said. "You should be tired. I'm surprised you didn't nap on the drive home."

"I enjoyed talking with you," she said.

Sean wondered what they'd talked about.

"I'll come with you, Zoe," Connie offered. "We can put your backpack in Sean's room."

Zoe's panicked expression returned, only this time she looked more uncomfortable than ever. "I, uh, can do it."

"I want to help," Connie said. "As Hank said, you're tired."

Sean inhaled sharply.

His mother was only trying to be open-minded. Modern. It was endearing, yet annoying since the one place Zoe wouldn't be sleeping was his room. He liked the thought of her in his bed, but she looked thoroughly embarrassed with her pink cheeks. "Zoe's staying in the guest bedroom, Mom."

Connie looked between him and Zoe. "Honey, there's no reason to pretend with us. You're both old enough to decide—"

"Guest bedroom."

His mother hesitated.

Hank picked up the backpack. "I'll take it upstairs."

"I'll get the pillows." The words were barely out of Zoe's mouth before she sprinted up the stairs.

Connie stared at Sean strangely. "You and Zoe—"

"She's not like other women, Mom," Sean admitted.

"I see that." Amusement and warmth reflected in his mother's eyes. "You know you're going to need help bathing."

He couldn't believe he was having this conversation. "We've got it covered, Mom."

"Your dad could always help."

Sean nodded, though sponge baths played a big role in his Nurse Zoe fantasy.

Connie opened the refrigerator. "Aunt Vera made you a casserole. I'll stick it in the oven for Zoe."

"Thanks, Mom." He remembered what she had said about her lack of cooking skills. "That will be really helpful since Zoe's so tired."

And he was hungry for something other than hospital food.

As his mother put the pan into the oven, Sean leaned his head back. The interviews, coming home. He was wiped out.

Zoe returned downstairs with her arms full of pillows. "Here you go."

Sean straightened. He could only see her jean-clad legs. Not a bad view actually. "I didn't realize I had that many pillows."

"I wasn't sure how many you needed," she said. "You might like a couple for your back so you don't get uncomfortable."

He smiled, knowing he could get away with more with his parents here. "That's what back massages are for."

"Massages, huh?" Zoe asked.

"Unless a sponge bath sounds better," Sean teased. He noticed his mother watching with interest. He'd behave when they were alone, but he would take advantage of their "relationship" when they were with his family and friends. A fair deal, he decided.

Zoe set all but one of the pillows on the couch next to him. She eyed him warily. "I'm hanging on to this in case I need to keep you in line."

"You wouldn't hit an injured man."

She narrowed her eyes playfully. "Are you willing to take that chance?"

Most definitely. He winked. "I can't forget about Popcorn."

Zoe blushed and lowered the pillow.

"Do you want some popcorn, Sean?" his mom asked.

"No, thanks."

"You don't play fair," Zoe whispered.

"I do when the odds are more even."

"When will that be?"

"Soon." He hoped.

As Zoe carefully placed pillows under his feet, his mother watched them. More than once she started to speak, but changed her mind. Sean felt as if he was fifteen again and bringing a girl home after school. It wasn't a good feeling.

"The timer will go off when Aunt Vera's casserole is ready," Connie announced. "I'll just get a salad and a couple of sides—"

"Come on, honey," Hank interrupted. "We've done our job here. It's time to go home and let the kids handle this."

Connie's gaze drifted to Sean. "But—"

"We'll be fine, Mom."

"He's in good hands, honey," his dad said gently.

Hank put his arm around Connie and led her to the door. She glanced back. "Call if you need anything."

"We will," Sean said.

His dad practically dragged her out of the house. The door slammed with a resounding thud.

"We're finally alone," Sean said.

"Massage or sponge bath?" Zoe teased.

His pulse picked up speed. "Can I have both?"

Mischief twinkled in her eyes. "If you're good."

"Oh, I'm very good."

"I'm sure you are." Zoe shielded herself with a pillow. "But don't forget I'm armed and mobile so watch out."

He smiled. "Trust me, I'm watching."

That was one homebound activity he was looking forward to.

She glanced toward the front door, her lips pressed together. "Do you think your parents are gone?"

The worry in her voice made him realize her flirting and playfulness had all been an act. Disappointed, he leaned against the couch. "They won't be back tonight. Relax. Make yourself at home."

She set the pillow on the couch. "Your house is lovely. Craftsman-style?"

He nodded.

"All the wood, glass, openness." She looked around. "The architecture fits the setting perfectly."

"Thanks." Sean was happy she liked the house. He patted the cushion next to him. "Sit."

She did.

"You did great," he said.

Zoe rolled her eyes. "Except for the pillows."

"Not a problem," he said. "People see what they want to see."

"What do your parents want to see?" Zoe asked.

"Grandchildren."

"So that explains why Connie wanted to put my backpack in your room."

"I'm not sure what explanation I have for that since she'd prefer a wedding to come first."

"Experience?"

He looked at her blankly.

"Lulu, Chelsea, Grace."

Sean wasn't going to touch that one. He didn't want to sound like a player. "My mom likes you."

"I like her." Zoe's eyes softened. "Connie loves you a lot. So does your dad."

"I know," Sean admitted. "They might drive me crazy, but I wouldn't trade them for anything."

"The feeling's mutual."

Sean shrugged. "Unfortunately for them."

Zoe laughed. "You're not that bad."

"Guess you'll find out."

She tilted her chin. "I'm looking forward to it."

So was he, Sean realized. A lot more than he should be.

CHAPTER FIVE

THE NEXT morning, gray light filtered through large wood-framed windows along the back wall of the house. Zoe yawned as she walked down the stairs. Afraid she might miss giving Sean his medication on time, she'd hardly slept. She hadn't wanted to make a mistake.

This was her first job. Zoe wouldn't let Sean down, or herself. So what if she was a little sleepy? She would grab a nap once Sean was awake and fed. That was why she hadn't changed out of her pajamas.

As Zoe stepped from the carpeted stair to the hardwood floor, she winced from the cold. It wasn't just the floor underneath her bare feet. The air temperature felt ten degrees cooler. She needed to adjust the thermometer. The last thing Sean needed was to catch a cold.

He lay asleep on the couch.

Zoe studied him.

The dawning light streamed down on his hair. His facial stubble made him look more rugged. His legs, elevated on pillows, were no longer covered. The blanket pooled on his chest. Still handsome, but he also looked a little…helpless.

She felt a pang.

Who was she kidding? He was helpless. Sean really needed someone. He needed her. The thought both pleased and terrified her at the same time.

She hadn't understood how much assistance he needed until helping him into the bathroom yesterday. Maneuvering his heavy, muscular body and the walker into the small space and waiting on the opposite side of the door for him to finish or call for help had been the definition of awkward. Sean had been even more embarrassed than her. The next time had been easier, but no less uncomfortable. Maybe in another day or so it would feel normal.

Zoe sure hoped so. She wanted Sean to feel normal again.

She'd never broken a bone in her body. She imagined it hurt both physically from the pain and emotionally due to the limitations forced upon a person. The limits had to be the hardest thing for Sean. Or would be shortly. He didn't seem like the type of guy to sit around all day. Last night, he'd almost damaged the remote channel-surfing to find something—anything—he was interested in watching.

She would have to keep him entertained, but how?

Zoe loved to snowboard. She worked out doing Zumba and Pilates, too. She was a decent athlete, but not the caliber of Sean, who climbed mountains and rescued people. Making his life during recovery less boring was going to be difficult. Her typical activities, at least before her banishment, had been shopping, dancing and partying.

What was she going to talk to him about? Suggest they do to keep him from getting restless being off his feet?

A lump the size of her Hermès coin purse formed in Zoe's throat. She took a deep, calming breath.

No reason to panic. Freaking out wouldn't help her get the job done. She shouldn't get ahead of herself. One day at a time. All she needed was a plan for this morning. She quickly decided what she should do: check on Sean, brew a pot of coffee and fix breakfast, give him his medicine, help him clean up and feed him. The only iffy thing was breakfast. Everything else she could handle. Even a sponge bath if that was what he needed.

A sponge bath.

The thought of touching a nearly naked Sean with a soapy sponge raised her temperature by fifteen degrees. She noticed the dark hair covering his leg and imagined running the palm of her hand over it.

What was she thinking?

Sean was her patient, her responsibility. Nothing more.

With her resolve and plan firmly in place, she walked quietly to the couch. Zoe adjusted the blanket so Sean's legs were covered. She expected him to bolt upright, but he didn't stir.

His eyes remained closed, his breathing even. The almost serene expression on his face made him look a decade younger, even with the appealing stubble. So handsome. She fought the urge to brush the hair hanging over his eye. No way did she want to risk waking him up and having to explain her actions.

Slowly, quietly, she backed away from him.

He continued sleeping.

See, Zoe told herself, her confidence gaining a needed boost. She could handle this.

In the kitchen, she checked the sheet of paper listing the doses of medication she'd given Sean. She still had time before his next round.

She had looked inside the cupboards last night so knew where to find the coffeemaker, filters and coffee. She opened a new package of coffee, scooped the already ground French roast beans into the filter, poured in the water and turned on the machine.

As the coffee brewed, Zoe stood at the kitchen island trying to figure out what to fix for breakfast. She glanced at Sean, who continued to sleep soundly.

Something moved in the backyard. She couldn't tell what, but it looked to be an animal of some sort.

A dog?

Oh, no. Zoe hoped it wasn't lost. The temperature had plummeted last night. Trying to get a closer look, she leaned over the counter until the granite counter pressed into her abdomen.

Not a dog. A deer. Make that two deer. They pranced across the yard like characters from *Bambi* come to life.

Excitement rushed through Zoe. She couldn't remember the last time she'd seen deer up close.

She raced to the back door, opened it slowly so the noise wouldn't startle the deer or wake Sean and stepped out onto the snow-covered deck.

The cold pierced her bare feet and seeped through her body. Zoe shivered, but she wasn't about to let the temperature send her back inside with the deer down below in the yard. She crossed her arms in front of her and wiggled her toes.

The scent of pine permeated the cold air. The smell brought back memories of Christmases past, of her father dressing up as Santa Claus and passing out gifts. She had always received the first gift from the large sack, as well as the last.

Tall evergreens, Douglas firs if she wasn't mistaken, formed an arc around a patch of snow dotted with hoof prints. A deer with velvet-covered antlers nibbled on some sort of vegetation. It might have even been bark.

She gasped in delight. Smiled.

The deer raised its head and looked at her. Its eyes looked cautious, yet bright.

So pretty.

Zoe stood transfixed, holding her breath. This wasn't something she saw, living in Los Angeles or even back home on the east coast. She was used to living in the city. Walking down Rodeo Drive in stilettos was the definition of hiking in her world. But this...

This was simply beautiful. The fresh air. Wildlife. Snow.

In spite of the cold temperature, warmth flowed through her. She'd forgotten how much she loved the mountains, a place her father had introduced her to before she could walk.

The setting here in Sean's backyard reminded Zoe of something out of a holiday movie. People in Hood Hamlet must feel like it was Christmas all winter long here. That must be so nice.

The deer broke eye contact and continued to chew. A doe, however, edged toward the trees, but stayed within sight.

Zoe watched in awe as the two explored the yard and ate. She couldn't believe she was experiencing this in person on Mount Hood and not sitting on the couch watching the scene unfold on the Animal Planet channel.

Talk about special.

As if on cue, large, fluffy snowflakes fell from the sky, spinning and dancing in their own choreography. Laughing, she raised her palms and caught an intricate flake. It melted almost on contact. Undeterred, she stuck out her tongue to catch another.

One landed in her mouth.

Nature's own snowcone. No flavoring needed.

Almost as tasty as Sean's kiss.

She grinned, wanting more, more snowflakes, more kisses. But kisses were too complicated. Sticking with snow was the smarter, safer option. She looked up at the sky and opened her mouth.

Warmth cocooned Sean as he lay on the sofa. He kept his eyes closed, ignoring the pressure in his legs and the crick in his back. He rarely slept in late, but drifting back asleep sounded like a good idea this morning. He'd been dreaming of riding powder with a pretty brunette with long hair.

Zoe.

As he pulled the blanket up under his chin so he could return to his dream, something tickled his nose. Coffee. Good coffee based on the robust aroma. After days of awful hospital sludge, the scent teased him fully awake. His dream would have to wait.

Sean opened his eyes.

Leave it to Zoe to know exactly how to kick off his first full day at home. A smile tugged at the corners of his lips.

Rising slightly on his elbows, he glanced toward the kitchen. No lights were on, but he saw the coffeemaker on the counter. Zoe wasn't there. He felt a twinge of disappointment. She must be upstairs.

The boot felt awkward. He adjusted one of the pillows beneath his left leg to get more comfortable.

The play of light and shadow through the wide glass windows snared his attention. He glanced outside at the falling snow and saw Zoe.

Zoe…dancing?

In her pajamas, a thin lavender tank and a pair of flannel bottoms. With her arms outstretched, she dipped and twirled.

Surrounded by falling snowflakes, she reminded him of a ballerina in a snow globe. Snow clung to her wet hair. She was barefoot, too.

He sat upright, ignoring the ache in his legs.

Showtime was over. She had to be freezing out there. That deck got slippery when wet. What if she fell?

"Zoe," he shouted, but she didn't hear him.

Sean reached for his walker. He wasn't comfortable using it yet, but Zoe needed to be inside where it was warm.

Standing up proved harder than Sean thought it would be. Twice he fell back on the couch, wincing. On the third try, he found his footing.

He ignored the dull throb in his legs. He tried to move faster, but couldn't. The muscles in his forearms strained as Sean supported himself with the walker. He steadied himself with one hand and opened the back door with the other.

Her bare feet stood on the snow-covered deck. Wet flannel clung to her skin, accentuating the curve of her hip and round bottom.

Sean grimaced, a combination of pain and arousal. "Zoe."

She swirled around, her eyes sparkling with excitement. Her wet lavender tank plastered against high, round breasts and beaded nipples. "Sean."

Desire hit hard and fast. The pressure in his legs was nothing compared to the ache in his groin. "Get inside before you freeze."

His voice sounded rough, on edge.

Zoe hurried into the house, closing the door behind her. Goose bumps covered her bare arms. The cotton, sticking to her body like a second skin, left nothing to his imagination.

She looked...really hot. And cold. Her wet feet left damp marks on the floor.

"Careful," he said huskily. "Don't slip."

"I didn't realize you were awake. You shouldn't be up." Concern filled Zoe's voice. "Are you in pain? You still have about fifteen minutes before you can take your medicine."

No medicine was going to help him now. His gaze continued to linger, his body responding to the memory of his dream and the closeness of her body. She smelled like woman and snow...

Cool it, Hughes.

She was living with him. She worked for him. He shouldn't leer. "Grab the blanket off the couch and warm yourself up."

"Let me make you breakfast—"

"Please, Zoe." Desperation filled his voice. Blood was rushing where he didn't want it to go. "For both our sakes."

Zoe wrapped the blanket around her shoulders. "Standing can't be good for you."

Lusting after his caretaker wasn't good for him, either. Sean hobbled to a chair, trying hard not to lose his balance, and sat. He felt immediate relief in his legs. If only he could get the same relief in other parts of his body.

Don't think about that, he told himself.

"You shouldn't be outside dressed like that." Sean put on his team leader face. "It's too cold. You could become hypothermic."

She raised her chin. "I appreciate the concern, but I wasn't out there that long."

"Long enough. Your pajamas are soaked through." And practically see-through, he thought.

Zoe opened the blanket and glanced down. "Oops."

He would have used another word.

She met his gaze with a rueful grin. "Well, I guess since I'll be seeing you half-dressed it's only fair you got to see a little of me."

He wanted to see a lot more. She had a killer body. She also had an easy confidence and humor that he liked a lot.

She shivered.

"You need to warm up," he said.

"A cup of coffee will do the trick." She retreated into the kitchen with the blanket around her. "Would you like one?"

"Please." He watched her pour coffee into two mugs. "What were you doing out there, anyway?"

"There were two deer in your backyard."

"Deer?"

"You know, Bambi," she explained.

Sean hadn't thought of Bambi since he was six. "There are lots of deer around here."

"Well, I'm not used to seeing them, so I went outside to get a closer look." A thoughtful smile formed on her lips. "Oh, Sean, you should have seen them. Velvety horns and dark eyes. Simply beautiful. And then all of a sudden, it started to snow. These perfect little snowflakes just floated down. I half expected to hear music play. It was that…"

Her wistful tone intrigued him. "What?"

She looked outside where snowflakes fell in a sheet of white. "Magical. The way Christmastime should be."

Zoe sounded like a Hallmark greeting card. Normally he hated sappy sentiments, but he found the words attractive coming from her.

"I'm sorry you had to come after me," she added.

"But you're not sorry for going outside to see the deer."

She pursed her lips. "No, I'm not."

He appreciated her honesty. "When Denali's here, deer keep their distance. But you should see a few more before she gets home," Sean said. "But next time you go outside put on shoes and a coat. A hat and gloves, too."

She nodded. "Do you want your coffee at the chair or couch?"

"The couch," he said. "But I'm going to wash up first."

As Sean stood, he felt off balance and nearly fell.

Zoe ran from the kitchen to his side. "I'll help."

"I've got it."

"I'm sure you do, but you have to be sore and your medication is wearing off. Don't forget, you're paying me to help. It wouldn't be right to accept a salary if I wasn't doing my job."

He'd hired her to keep his parents off his back more than to play nursemaid. "Suit yourself."

Zoe didn't say a word, but remained with him. When he reached the bathroom, Sean negotiated himself inside with less effort than it had taken last night. Not a lot of progress, but he'd take it.

At the sink, he stared at the row of toiletries laid out conveniently on the counter: washcloth, towel, shaving cream, razor, toothbrush, toothpaste and comb. He stared at Zoe. "You did this."

She nodded. "Last night."

Her actions touched him. "Thanks."

"Let's get your shirt off."

His temperature spiked higher. He gripped the handles of the walker. He wanted her to undress him. And he wanted to undress her. But…

"Don't be modest," she said.

Sean pressed the walker and himself close to the sink. She must have no idea what she was doing to him. Or maybe she did. He glanced at her. No, she didn't seem the type to purposely tease a man. All she wanted to do was help him.

Maybe her help would extend past her caretaker duties. He'd be game. "Go ahead."

Zoe tucked the blanket under her arms. As she raised the hem of his T-shirt, her knuckles grazed his skin. His tingling nerve endings stood at alert.

"Let's try one hand at a time," she suggested.

He let go of the walker with his left hand and pulled it through the armhole.

"Other one," she said.

He did and soon stood shirtless with Zoe right behind him.

She tilted her chin. "Was that so hard?"

He shook his head, not trusting his voice.

Awareness buzzed through him. He tried to think of something to kill his attraction, but all he could see was Zoe in her wet pajamas. He swallowed.

"What's next?"

"I can handle the rest," Sean said between clenched teeth. Not even the blanket was keeping his fantasies at bay. He needed her to go away and get dressed ASAP.

"Go change into dry clothes," he added. "And can you grab me some clean clothes to put on while you're upstairs? Shorts and T-shirts are in my dresser."

"I can't leave you alone."

"I'll be fine."

"I don't—"

"I need clothes to wear." He was losing his patience.

"Okay." She lowered the toilet seat cover. "I'll run upstairs if you promise to sit here until I return."

"Zoe."

"Sean."

He needed to get her out of here before she realized the effect she was having on him, so he sat.

"I'm leaving the door cracked," she said.

She acted as if she was his babysitter, not a woman attracted to a man. "Is that necessary?"

"Yes, and I promise I won't peek," she said lightheartedly.

"You're more polite than me."

Smart, Zoe, really smart.

Upstairs, she peeled off her wet pajamas. She really needed to think before she acted.

Zoe dried off with a towel from the upstairs bathroom, stepped into a pair of panties and clasped her bra.

Seeing the deer had made her happy. Sean, however, didn't look happy with her at all. At least he hadn't chastised her like her mother had when those photos of her topless at a beach on the Côte d'Azur made the rounds in the tabloids and on the Internet this summer.

She pulled a sweater over her head.

Still, this wasn't the impression she wanted to make with him. Sean hadn't hidden his interest. She was interested in him, too. And she hadn't had to take off his T-shirt and see his muscular chest and abs to realize it.

But she would have to ignore the physical attraction between them. She had to be responsible. She was Sean's caretaker, his pretend girlfriend. Anything more would be a really bad idea.

She only hoped he agreed.

Sean.

Zoe needed to get back downstairs pronto. She wiggled into a pair of jeans, pulled on a pair of socks and rushed into Sean's bedroom. She'd been in such a hurry getting the pillows and later his toiletries, she hadn't taken a good look at his room before.

A navy blue comforter covered a king-size bed. The nightstands and dresser matched the slotted headboard. A painting of Mount Hood hung on the wall. A digital alarm clock and lamp set on one of the nightstands. Books—*Freedom of the Hills, Classic Climbs of the Northwest*—and a snowboarding magazine were stacked on the other.

Masculine, yet comfortable.

A lot like Sean.

Zoe opened his top drawer to find neatly folded underwear—boxer-briefs and boxers. She grabbed a pair of green plaid ones. The next drawer contained socks, which she took even though he hadn't asked for any. Another had T-shirts so she grabbed a white one. In the bottom drawer, she found a pair of navy shorts.

She returned downstairs.

Things had not gone well so far. Zoe had to put the morning behind her and show Sean she could take care of him. Looking on the bright side, at least things could only go up from here.

Sean sat in the bathroom, waiting. His heart pounded against his ribs.

Forget the injuries to his legs and head. Zoe was the one who would do him in.

Ignoring her order to stay seated, he awkwardly positioned himself in front of the sink and splashed cold water on his face. A cold shower would be better, but he didn't have that option. At least washing off would cool him down and help get himself back together.

A mix of emotions swirled through him.

Anger, annoyance, arousal.

You know, Bambi.

Amusement.

Sean laughed. He couldn't be upset at Zoe. She'd admitted she was impulsive. He'd just experienced it in action. Life would never be boring with her. That was for sure.

He liked her. He appreciated her thoughtfulness at setting out his toiletries. He liked the way little things, such as wildlife or snowfall, excited her. She made him smile and feel better. He wanted to return the favor though he wasn't sure how to do that.

Maybe in a couple of days when he felt better he could convince her to play doctor. He grinned. Her impulsiveness could turn out to be a good thing in the long run.

He caught his reflection in the mirror and frowned.

Damn. Even after three weeks of climbing in Patagonia, he hadn't looked *this* grungy. Sean combed his fingers through his hair. It didn't help.

Forget playing doctor. Zoe wasn't going to want to be anywhere near him. Ignoring the throbbing in his legs, Sean brushed his teeth.

No pain, no gain. The phrase summed up ice climbing, where scaling a waterfall of ice in the biting cold made calves whine and shoulder and back muscles burn. The words fit his situation now.

Sean balanced his weight by resting a hip against the walker. He rubbed shaving cream on his face and ran the razor across the whiskers.

"You're supposed to be sitting down."

Uh-oh. Zoe didn't sound happy.

Sean turned to the sound of her voice. She stood in the doorway with his clothes in the crook of her arm. A green V-neck sweater fit tightly across her chest and her jeans accentuated the curve of her hips.

The air in the bathroom seemed to crackle with attraction.

Forcing himself not to stare, Sean rinsed his razor. "I have to look in the mirror to shave."

"You shouldn't be standing."

"You shouldn't be peeking."

She gave his bare chest the once-over. Approval filled her eyes. He stood taller.

"I couldn't help myself," she said after a long moment.

That brought another smile to his face. Maybe Zoe liked scruffy, rugged types. "Irresistible, huh?"

Her assessing gaze made him feel as if he were under a microscope. "Not really."

He nearly nicked his face. Women usually flocked to him. "You like pretty boys."

"If you were any prettier, you'd have to change your name to Shauna," Zoe said. "It has nothing to do with how you look. I know being injured must be hard, but if you're not careful you could fall and hurt yourself more. I don't want that to happen."

"I can take care of myself," he said stiffly.

"Then you don't need me."

She was stronger than he expected. Smarter, too. He'd played right into her hand.

"I do." He repositioned the walker and sat. "I just…" The concern on her face made him feel like a jerk. "I'm used to being the one helping people."

"You are helping," she said. "You're helping me."

He looked down at his useless legs. "Yeah, right."

"It's true."

Sean didn't need her pity. "I have no problem relying on climbing partners when I'm on the mountain or at a crag. There I can pull my own weight. But here…"

In his own home. In the bathroom.

He shook his head.

"Let's talk about here. At your house and at the hospital. You gave me a job." Zoe touched his shoulder. Her warm, soft skin sent a burst of heat rushing through him.

"A job to keep me from having to live with my parents."

She shrugged. "That's one way to look at it. We might be using each other, but we're also helping each other. The day we met, Thanksgiving, I only had enough money to buy a lift ticket or food, not both. I had no idea where I would go next or what I would eat that day."

"Yet you decided to ride."

Zoe nodded, her eyes dark. "I chose one family Thanksgiving tradition over another. Not the most financially responsible decision I've ever made."

"It's a decision I would have made if I'd been in your shoes," he admitted. "Actually I have made that same decision when I was younger."

Except Sean had a family he could fall back on, a family that would have never let him go hungry even if he spent every dollar he made on snowboarding and starting his own company.

He remembered what she'd said about being estranged from her family. She must really miss them if she wanted to keep their traditions alive so badly she would go hungry. "So what's the deal with your family?"

She shrugged.

"You miss them."

"Sometimes," she admitted. "But I don't miss being judged. My mother and brothers…"

Sean wondered about her father. "What?"

"Nothing."

He didn't press, even though he was curious. He respected her privacy. She would tell him more when she was ready.

"Anyway," she continued, "I'm really happy I chose to ride that day because I got to meet you. You gave me a lift, an invite to dinner, a job and a place to stay. H-E-L-P, in case you need me to spell it out for you."

Sean hadn't thought of it that way. "I can see your point."

"Good." Her smile widened. "Now maybe you'll let me do something for you."

Her generosity of spirit—and her offer—took his breath away. He could think of lots of things he wanted her to do for him. "What did you have in mind?"

She blushed. "How about breakfast?"

Baby steps. That was what the doctor had said. The same strategy applied to Zoe. Sean grinned. "I am hungry. Maybe you could fix us both something while I finish washing up."

Zoe pursed her lips. "Promise me you won't get up again."

"Promise."

She placed his clothes over a towel rack. "Give me a shout out when you're ready to get dressed. I'll leave the door cracked so I can hear you."

Remaining seated, Sean washed off. He heard pans bang together in the kitchen. Not wanting to be an even bigger burden, he struggled to change out of his clothes.

He managed to get his basketball shorts and boxers off, but getting dressed wasn't so easy. With the boxers tucked inside the shorts, he brought the waistband over his feet, but he couldn't get his foot through the leg openings.

He cursed, tried again, swore. His elbow hit something off the counter. The shaving cream can clattered against the floor.

"Sean?" Zoe called.

Damn. He was naked. Sean covered his lap with a towel.

She poked her head into the bathroom. "Are you okay?"

He pointed to the shaving cream on the floor. "I knocked the can over."

Zoe stared at the clothes lying on the floor. "You were trying to get dressed yourself."

Looking down, he nodded.

"This is a two person job." She kneeled in front of him. Quickly she rolled his shorts and boxers into a roll. "It's no different than putting on panty hose."

"I wouldn't know."

"A good thing you have me then."

She was eye level with his knees. As she bent over, he had a perfect view straight down the neckline of her sweater. He could see the V of her breasts, ivory skin, white lace.

Sweat broke out on his upper lip.

One leg at a time she brought up the shorts. Her hands brushed his feet. Her hair caressed his leg. "See, this isn't so bad."

Maybe not for her.

She raised the roll up to his knees. "Almost there."

No kidding. Sean swore under his breath. He was getting turned-on. Again. He placed his hands on his lap. "I can take it from here," he said, desperate for her to leave him alone again.

"Now the socks," she said.

"I don't wear socks in the house."

"Your feet will get cold."

"I could slip."

"You—"

A loud squeal sounded. An obnoxious sound that hurt his brain. What the—

Panic crossed Zoe's face. "Breakfast."
She ran out of the bathroom.
The smoke detector.
Oh, hell.

CHAPTER SIX

SEAN ripped off the towel, lifted his hips off the seat and tugged up the waistbands of his shorts and boxers. In spite of the blare of the alarm, he heard clanging and doors opening.

"Ouch," Zoe cried.

Clutching the handles, Sean threw the walker in front of him. He stood only to be forced down again by the pain in his leg. He tried again, but this time focused on Zoe. It worked. He stayed on his feet.

When he reached the doorway, Sean smelled smoke.

Adrenaline shot through his veins.

Out of the bathroom, he noticed the front door wide open. He hobbled into the great room. Zoe used a towel to fan the smoke out the back door and windows.

"Zoe?"

She looked at him. "I've got everything under control."

The alarm silenced.

He made his way across the floor and eased onto the couch before his legs gave out. "What happened?"

She continued fanning. "Cooking challenged, remember?"

"Yeah, I remember." Something smoldered in the kitchen sink. "Is that…breakfast?"

"It was, but caught fire when I was—"

"In the bathroom with me."

"I'm sorry." She sounded frustrated. "This really hasn't been a good morning."

"Zoe."

Instead of looking at him, she kept waving the towel, trying to clear the smoke.

"You must be freezing." She closed the back door. "You need a sweatshirt and a clean blanket—"

"Zoe," he repeated. "Slow down. It's okay."

"But it's not. I should be handling this better. My mother really was right."

"About you being impulsive?"

"And a few other things."

"I'm willing to take my chances."

"What if the fire had been worse?" Zoe glanced toward the kitchen. "You might not have been able to get out."

"It wasn't that bad."

She bit her lip. "This time."

Sean hoped it was the last time. He rubbed his aching leg.

"Oh, no." She sprinted to the kitchen, filled a glass with water and opened pill containers. "It's past time for your meds."

"I'm fine."

She returned to the couch, handed him the water and medicine. "The doctor said you're supposed to stay ahead of the pain."

He swallowed the pills. "How late am I taking the medicine?"

"Twelve minutes."

"No worries."

Tears glistened in her eyes. "I really wanted to do well here."

Something twisted inside of him at the regret in her voice. He shoved a pillow off the couch. "Sit."

She did.

"It's okay," he said.

"Okay?" She stared at him. "If the rest of the day continues like this morning, you'll catch pneumonia and be dead by nightfall."

"I'll give Popcorn your regards."

Tears fell from the corners of her eyes.

Damn. He'd wanted to make her smile, not cry.

Sean wrapped his arm around her. She felt nice and warm against his bare chest. But this was about Zoe, not him. "Don't worry about it."

She sniffled.

He pulled her closer.

"It's your first day. First days are always the hardest." The scent of grapefruit filled his nostrils. Sean felt dizzy. He wasn't sure if it was Zoe or the medicine. "Remember what I said about ordering takeout?"

He felt her nod.

"We can get breakfast to go."

Zoe looked up at him with a confused look in her eyes. "You're not angry at me?"

"Not at all."

"But so much has gone wrong. You're supposed to be off your feet, not running around and catching a chill because of me." The words tumbled from her mouth in a rush. "I'm really not quali—"

Sean pressed his lips against hers. Zoe stiffened, no doubt as surprised by his kiss as he was. But it was the only way he knew how to stop her from talking and getting more upset.

He expected her to back away. She didn't. Instead, Zoe kissed him back. Her soft breasts pressed against him, heating the blood pounding through his veins.

He moved his lips over hers, tasting and touching and exploring. Something he hadn't been able to do at the hospital. Something he enjoyed doing now. She fit so nicely against him.

As Zoe wove her fingers through his hair, she took the kiss deeper.

Wow. She really was a good kisser.

A noise sounded. Lots of noise actually, but Sean didn't

want to stop kissing her. He would be happy to spend the rest of the day with her on the couch.

"What the...?"

The sound of a male voice made Sean jerk back from Zoe. He looked over and saw members of the Hood Hamlet Fire Department standing in his kitchen and great room.

"Looks like the fire's out," Bill Paulson, also an OMSAR member, said.

Leanne Thomas grinned. "I'd say it's just heating up."

Sean had climbed with both of them during OMSAR missions and for fun. Great climbing partners and even closer friends. He knew them well enough to know they were never going to let him live this down. Rightly so, since Sean would do the same if he was standing in their places.

"Did you dial 911?" he asked Zoe.

Red-cheeked, she shook her head.

"No one called," Bill explained. "Remember that state-of-the-art alarm system I told you to install?"

"Damn."

Leanne nodded. "A neighbor heard the alarm and saw smoke so she called, too."

More firefighters entered.

Zoe cringed. "I'm so sorry."

Sean squeezed her shoulder.

"What happened?" Bill asked.

"I tried to cook breakfast," she answered before Sean could. "I don't cook."

Bill gave her an appreciative once-over. "Cooking's over-rated."

Christian Welton and John Keller nodded.

Leanne rolled her eyes.

"Sorry about the false alarm," Sean said. "You guys must have better things to do with your time."

Christian, who was the rookie at the station and could red-point 5.13 routes at Smith Rock, stared at Zoe like a lovesick puppy. "I'd rather be here than sitting at the station."

Sean wanted him and all the rest of the crew gone so he

could be alone with Zoe and kiss her again. "Do what you need to do so you can get out of here."

"May I see your hand, Zoe?" Leanne asked.

Her hand? Sean looked at Zoe.

She hid it behind her back. "Oh, it's nothing."

Sean's muscles tensed. "What's wrong with your hand?"

She smiled at him. "Just a little burn."

Oh, hell. A burn. He hadn't even thought... "Let me see."

"I'll take care of it." Leanne led Zoe away.

He tried to stand, but Bill stopped him. "Don't get in the way, Hughes. You know she's in good hands."

Leanne had patched Sean up more than once, but that didn't make this any easier. He was used to being in the center of the action, usually in charge of a rescue team. He didn't like being on this side of things. He hated not being able to see what Leanne and the other paramedic, Marc, were doing to Zoe.

"Status?" Sean asked as soon as they had finished.

The other firefighters surrounded Zoe. Bill dealt with the smoldering mess in the sink.

"Nothing serious. A first degree burn." Leanne walked over to Sean and lowered her voice. "It's obvious the two of you are crazy about each other, but Zoe needed First Aid more than she needed a kiss. Even one of your kisses, Hughes."

Okay, his mind had been on other things, but why hadn't Zoe told him she'd burned herself? "I'll pay more attention to her."

Leanne laughed. "Any more attention, and you'll enter creepy-stalker zone."

Sean frowned.

"Kidding, and you should know that." Leanne's forehead creased. "I had no idea you were seriously dating someone, but it's about time. Does Zoe climb?"

"No, but she wants to."

"You going to teach her to cook, too?" Leanne winked.

"Though I'm guessing the kitchen is the last room you want Zoe to spend her time."

"Guilty as charged."

"Just don't add her to the long list of hearts you've broken." Leanne was one of the guys, but every once in a while her feminine side peeked out. "I talked to Zoe at the hospital. She seems sweet. Nice. I like her."

Leanne wasn't the only one. The guys swarmed around Zoe as if she was the queen bee and they were her drones.

"And you look better already," Leanne added. "She's good for you."

"I'd like to keep her around." He understood the attention Zoe was receiving, but he didn't like it. Time to send Hood Hamlet's finest back to where they came from. "You think you can get all these babe-magnets away from my girl?"

"They're filling out the report."

"All of them?" he asked.

"They like pretty things."

"Tell you what," Sean said. "If you can clear them out of here, I'll let you have the first lead when I'm back climbing."

"You're on." Leanne grinned with anticipation. "Come on, boys. Finish up the paperwork. It's time to head back to the station."

The firefighters shuffled out of the kitchen with a chorus of goodbyes and long glances back at Zoe. The front door slammed shut.

She blew out a puff of air. "So…"

He focused on her bandaged hand. "Why didn't you tell me you were burned?"

She shrugged. "I want to do a good job."

"But if you're hurt…"

"It's nothing," she said. "You must be starving."

Zoe was trying to change the subject. Again.

"I am." But not for breakfast. In spite of her burn, he wanted to kiss her again. The way her gaze kept drifting to his lips made him think she wanted the same thing. Good, another thing they agreed on. Not that he usually had a lot in common with the women he went out with. Casual dating didn't require that. "Come over here so we can get back to what we were doing."

The thought of kissing Sean again filled Zoe's stomach with butterflies. Kissing him made her forget all her troubles. It also made her forget all the reasons she couldn't get involved in any sort of relationship with him.

Thank goodness the Hood Hamlet Fire Department had showed up. They had stopped her from making another impulsive mistake.

Yes, she liked kissing Sean. He made her feel special. But even bruised and with both legs injured, he was dangerous to her new resolve.

She had to stand her ground. "I...we can't."

He flashed her a dazzling grin that made her knees go weak. "Yes, we can."

"I mean, it's not a good idea," she said firmly. "You need me to help you more than you need me to kiss you."

"I know what I need. I have a pretty good idea what you need, too." Mischief gleamed in his eyes. "Trust me, we can do both."

She could—a part of her was tempted to give in to his charm—but... "More kisses would complicate things."

"What things?" he asked.

"Us. Not that there's an 'us,'" she backtracked, not wanting to read anything more into the kiss than what it had been. She liked him. But earlier, when she'd talked about them using and helping each other, kissing was not what she had in mind. "We can't get physical. Whatever we've told your family and friends, we're practically strangers."

"I don't think of you that way," he said. "But even if I did, what better way to get to know each other?"

The anticipation in his eyes made her pulse quicken. She felt her resolve weakening.

Zoe squared her shoulders. "What if we did get involved, and it didn't work out? It would be awful. I'd have to leave."

"You're going to be leaving anyway."

"When you don't need me anymore." The thought made her sad for reasons she didn't want to examine.

Sean eyed her warily. "Is that a problem?"

"Leaving, no." She needed to get a grip. "As long as my job is finished here, and we're not personally involved."

"We're both adults," he countered.

"So we have to act like adults." She cringed. "Oh, no, I sound just like my mother."

"And that's a bad thing."

"Usually, because my mother is a very controlled, cautious, responsible person."

"Then don't be like your mother and come here."

Temptation grew. But as Zoe took a step toward Sean, her mother's warnings about men and love returned with renewed force. She had never listened before and look where that had gotten her. She stopped five feet from Sean. "You know, sometimes my mother is right. She only has my best interests at heart. And I only have yours."

He stared at her, in disbelief or confusion Zoe couldn't be certain, but she knew what she had to do.

"No more kissing," Zoe said in case he didn't get the point.

From the set of his jaw, she could see Sean did, and he didn't like it.

No more kissing.

Sean wasn't happy about not kissing Zoe, but he had to respect her new rule. And he did. Sort of. He didn't kiss her again when they were alone. But when people dropped by to visit often during the next two days, and whenever they had an audience, he snagged as many kisses as he could.

A jerk move? Probably.

But he liked kissing Zoe. And even though he knew she

was playing a role for others, she seemed to like kissing him, too.

He couldn't understand why she didn't want to take things between them to the next level. They already spent all their time with each other. Why not be together in every sense of the word?

Her restrictions chafed. He was already frustrated. His energy was improving. He didn't need as many pain pills. And he was desperate to get back to work.

At least he had his laptop.

Sean stared at the screen. The words blurred. Must be glare from the screen. He squinted. It didn't help.

He'd been going through the hundreds of e-mails that had piled up in his in-box. Maybe he should do something else.

He opened a file about the Rail Jam Extravaganza, an upcoming PR event he needed to attend at New Year's.

As he read the information, a sharp pain sliced through his head. He massaged his forehead.

"That's enough." Zoe walked toward him. "You said you wanted to check e-mail, but you've been online working for three solid hours."

She grabbed his laptop.

He reached for it, but she was too quick and backed away. "Hey, I need that," he said.

"You're squinting and have a headache. In case you forgot, you have a concussion. I'm going to have to restrict your computer usage so you won't overdo it again."

"I won't overdo it."

She hugged the laptop to her chest. "You won't now."

"I have a company to run."

"I have a job to do," she said. "You can ask your doctor about working full-time when you have your sutures removed."

"That's—"

"How it's going to be." Zoe moved toward the built-in shelving unit. "I'll put this away, then we can watch that DVD your mom dropped off."

Knowing his mom, it would probably be a love story, a romantic comedy where the guy proposes at the end. Subtlety was not in Connie Hughes's vocabulary.

Zoe bent over to set the laptop back in its place. Her scoop top provided a great flash of her round, high breasts. Was that a hot-pink bra?

Sean blew out his breath. He needed to show her that kissing each other would be a lot more fun than playing games and watching movies. He shifted to get a better view and elbowed a can of soda onto the floor. Brown liquid splattered on the hardwood floor.

Zoe straightened. "You okay?"

"Fine, but I made a mess."

She grabbed a roll of paper towels. "I'll clean it up."

He hated that his leering had been the cause of all this. "It would be easier with a mop."

"A mop?"

"In the laundry room."

"The laundry room," she repeated. "Where else would a mop be?"

Zoe returned in a few minutes with a mop and a bucket. She filled the bucket with water at the kitchen sink. "Do you use soap on the floor?"

Hadn't she mopped a floor before? Maybe not hardwoods.

"My mom says a little dishwashing soap goes a long way," he said.

"Right."

Sean turned on the television set and flipped through the channels. So many stations yet nothing good ever seemed to be on. Truth was, he'd rather watch Zoe.

She carried the bucket to the spill. As she stuck in the mop, water cascaded over the edges. "Guess I put in a little too much water."

He didn't say anything. It was his fault she had to mop the floor in the first place. He changed the channel again so she wouldn't think he was staring at her.

She tucked her hair behind her ears, pulled the mop out of the water and swabbed the spill. Water flew everywhere, making an even bigger mess.

First a fire, now a flood. Sean bit back a smile. It was always entertaining with her around.

Staring at all the water, Zoe leaned against the mop with a dejected look on her face.

He remembered what Zoe had said to him at the hospital.

I'm not, uh, very domestic. I feel it's fair to warn you I'm cooking and cleaning challenged.

In spite of his headache, Sean tried to piece together the clues she'd given him about her past. Snowboarding on Thanksgiving with her family. That would be expensive. Her board and outfit weren't cheap, knockoff brands, either. Yet Zoe had told him she'd been running low on funds and didn't have a place to live. She couldn't cook or clean, either. Zoe Flynn might not have money herself, but he'd bet her family did. Sean wanted to know more about her.

"Sorry you have to clean up after me," he said.

"That's okay."

"I'm not used to it," he said. "Somebody else cleaning up my mess."

She didn't reply.

He tried again. "I guess you're used to having a housecleaner."

A smile broke over her face. "In college, I even paid my roommate to clean and do my laundry."

Definitely from money, Sean realized. That explained a few things.

She bit her lip, as if realizing she'd said too much. "So where did I go wrong? With the floor?"

Apparently more revelations would have to wait. "You need to squeeze the water out of the mop before you try to wipe the floor with it."

"So that's what that thingy at the bottom is for."

He grinned. "Yeah."

She put the mop over the bucket and wrung the water out of it with the lever. "You learn something new every day."

Sean nodded thoughtfully. He couldn't wait to learn more about Zoe. Most women didn't shut up about themselves, but Zoe diverted his questions. That raised his curiosity and his concern.

What was she hiding? Or who was she hiding from?

A few days later, Zoe pushed her stack of poker chips forward. "All in."

Her move didn't seem to surprise Sean. Well, if it did, she couldn't tell. His expression remained exactly the same as it had been all through the game. He studied the flop, turn and river cards lying between them on the couch.

On the radio, Mariah Carey sang "All I Want For Christmas Is You." Zoe knew what she wanted. Not for Christmas, but right now.

She wanted to win.

Sean reminded her of a border collie, a high energy animal that didn't like being kenneled or leashed or, in Sean's case, stuck on the couch. He'd been right saying this wasn't an easy job. Helping Sean and not letting him try to do too much was a full-time job. Not to mention doing chores around the house.

Worse, she'd been struggling to keep him from getting bored. Bored equaled grumpy so she'd tried to keep him busy playing video games, board games and anything else she could think of. He'd been counting the days until he could get his computer back. But when she'd found a silver case full of poker chips and cards in the coat closet, her job had gotten easier because Sean loved playing poker. That improved his mood.

His healing seemed to be taking care of itself, but everyone from Connie to Jake Porter said Zoe was the reason. She wasn't going to take all the credit, but the compliments filled her with pride. She was finally doing something right and being responsible. Her mother would be pleased, but that didn't matter as much to Zoe now. She was necessary to Sean in a way she'd never been necessary to anyone before. She'd never felt so valued or valuable and didn't want it to end anytime soon.

Zoe studied her cards. "You could always fold."

Sean raised an eyebrow. "Having second thoughts?"

"None whatsoever."

And Zoe didn't. She was going to win. Finally. She had three aces—two in her hand and one in the river position.

"Such confidence," he said.

She searched for any kind of tell that would give away his cards, but nothing in his mannerisms and facial expression told her if he was bluffing or holding a winning hand. "It's all in the cards."

Sean's gaze met hers, probing yet secretive. She stared back, as if she could will him to call her bet.

The air sizzled between them.

Slowly, his fingers inched toward his stacks of chips that towered over hers.

Zoe's heart beat faster. The game, she told herself, not him and how much healthier and happier he looked today. If she didn't win this hand, she would be out.

He matched the amount of chips she'd put in. "Call."

With a smile, she turned over her cards. "Three aces."

Sean flipped his. A two, three, four, five, six.

Her shoulders sagged. "I don't believe it. A straight."

Using his hand, he swept the pile of chips toward him. "We're different kinds of players."

She gathered the deck of cards. "Yeah, you win."

Sean's smile crinkled the corners of his eyes.

Butterflies flapped in her stomach. She focused on this pile of chips.

"That's not quite what I meant," he explained. "You play by instinct. That means you'll win big, but you'll also lose big. It's an exciting way to play if you don't mind taking the risks."

"You're the risk taker, not me." Zoe tucked the cards

into their box. "You climb mountains, snowboard, rescue people."

"I take calculated risks. Ones I'm prepared for."

"And I just go all in."

"That makes you fun to play with," he said.

"Easy to beat."

Laughter gleamed in his eyes. "That, too."

"So how do you decide when you're going to bet?"

He sorted the chips. "I only bet when I'm going to win."

She thought about the times he folded or checked. "So if you don't think you can win…"

"I don't play."

"And I only play harder," she said. "We do approach the game differently."

He nodded. "The way a person plays cards says a lot about them."

No kidding. Sean played to win. His MO extended beyond poker and reaffirmed her decision not to kiss him again. Well, except for pecks on the cheek in front of his family and friends. Losing a card game was one thing, but having her heart broken was something to be avoided at all costs.

"Want to play again?" he asked.

"Not now," she said. "You know all my secrets."

He grinned. "I wouldn't say all of them."

Sean was right, and Zoe had to keep it that way. She chewed the inside of her cheek.

"But I'm hoping to discover a few more," he added.

Panic bolted through her. "You might be disappointed by what you learn."

"No way. Not after all that you've done for me."

Thank goodness. A way to change the subject. Talking about herself made Zoe uncomfortable. She didn't want to lie to Sean, yet couldn't tell him the whole truth, either. "You're doing so much better."

"Thanks to you."

Her cheeks warmed. "Just doing my job."

"A good job, but I can't wait until I can shower."

"I could try taping plastic bags over your feet and legs."

"That's okay," he said. "I'm still working on negotiating the stairs with the walker. The sutures come off soon. I can wash up at the sink a few days longer."

She couldn't do much about his desire to shower, but she could make one thing easier for him. "Want me to wash your hair?"

"I don't mind ducking it under the faucet."

"But I mind. Please let me do this for you."

"I'd rather play another round of poker."

"If you let me wash your hair, I'll play another game after dinner."

Not that she had much to do to prepare the food. Once word got out about her lack of cooking skills, meals appeared every day. Zoe only had to order takeout occasionally now. She would have liked to learn to cook for Sean, but this was better for him and kept the fire department away.

"Deal," he said.

Zoe was relieved he was up for something new. She only hoped this activity would go off without a hitch unlike some of the others. She stood. "I'll be right back."

CHAPTER SEVEN

TEN MINUTES later, Zoe had everything in place. Towels padded the edge of the granite counter. A bar stool set in front of the sink. A bottle of shampoo was within arm's reach. "Ready?"

"Not really." He made his way toward her using the walker. "Playing beauty salon isn't really my thing."

"You have no idea what you're missing out on." She helped him sit in the chair and moved his walker out of the way. "Take off your shirt."

"Is being shirtless a prerequisite for getting your hair washed?"

"It'll keep your shirt from getting soaked."

His eyes brightened as he pulled off his T-shirt. "Do I get to wash your hair next?"

"No."

He shrugged. "A guy sometimes has to try."

"And a girl sometimes has to say no." Even when she had to force her gaze from drifting downward to his bare chest and abs. She adjusted the towels to better cushion his head. "Comfortable?"

"Fine."

Zoe removed the nozzle, hit the spray button and tested the water against her wrist. "Relax."

"I'm relaxed."

The moment the warm water hit Sean's head, his eyes widened. She ran her hand over his hair. Strands of hair slipped through her fingers. Slowly, his eyelids drooped.

"Feel good?" she asked.

"Mmm-hmm."

She squeezed shampoo onto her palm and rubbed it on his head. Slowly she worked the shampoo into his hair. The rise and fall of his chest became more even, calm.

Leaning over to reach the back of his head, her breasts brushed his arm. She jerked back. "Sorry."

"No worries."

Zoe wished she could say the same. The water temperature matched the heat emanating from Sean's body. She felt as if the thermostat had been turned up fifteen degrees. The turtleneck she wore only made her hotter.

"So this is what I've been missing by going to a barber all these years," he said, his eyes nearly closing. "No wonder women get their hair done so much."

She rubbed her fingertips against his scalp to work up a lather. The scent of coconut filled her nostrils. "I love going to the salon. A new cut. A different color. It's like I'm a new person when I walk out the door."

Sean's gaze fixed on her face. "I like the person you are just fine."

His words would have pleased her, except he didn't know the truth about her. "You don't know me very well."

"Well enough." As if sensing her discomfort, he lightened his tone. "So what's your natural color?"

Water spurted. "Oh. Um. I hardly remember. I've been coloring my hair since I was fifteen."

"Fifteen?"

She nodded. "My mother didn't want me to so I couldn't go to a salon. A friend and I did it by ourselves. My hair turned green."

"I can't imagine you with green hair."

"I once streaked it with hot-pink-and-blue stripes," Zoe admitted. "That was my alternative rock stage. I also went through a Goth stage in high school. The jet-black hair drove my mother absolutely insane."

Sean studied her face. "I don't see any body piercings."

"My mother would have killed me if I'd done that. I had to make do with black nail polish and temporary tattoos."

Zoe massaged his scalp. His wet hair slid through her hands. His scalp felt smooth beneath the pads of her fingers.

"You're way too sweet to be into that look," he said.

She shrugged. "Sometimes I wasn't so sweet."

Sean raised a brow. "Are your brothers as rebellious?"

"Not at all."

"How many brothers?"

"Three. Older," she added, forestalling his next question. "And they always did, still do, what Mother wanted."

Clean-cut and conservative, her brothers had accumulated advanced degrees, high-paying jobs, beautiful wives and perfectly groomed children in the appropriate order and according to their mother's timetable. Maxwell, the oldest one, had recently run and won a seat in the state legislature.

Zoe grimaced. "I haven't been so good at meeting expectations."

"Me, either," Sean said.

She looked down at him in surprise. No one could say Sean wasn't successful. "In what way?"

"Well, my dad would have preferred if I'd gone into the construction business with him. And let's not even mention children. Rather the lack of them."

She laughed.

"You haven't mentioned your father," Sean said.

Remembered warmth settled around Zoe's heart. "My father was the greatest. Friendly and fun—that was my dad."

"He sounds like you."

"My mother says I'm a lot like him." She ran her fingers over his scalp again. "He died when I was twelve. A heart attack."

"I'm sorry."

Zoe nodded. "Things were never the same after he was gone. But I think he would have liked all my different hair colors. Even the wild, crazy ones."

Sean reached up and tucked a strand of hair behind her ear. "I like your hair now."

"Thanks." She picked up the spray nozzle. "My mother actually suggested it."

"Before you were estranged?"

Zoe nodded.

"You said you missed them."

"Yes, but…" How could she explain to him that she needed this time away? Not only to spare her mother's campaign, but also to figure out what she wanted. "I'm happy I'm here with you."

"So am I."

His words gave her a boost of confidence.

"So you're the youngest," Sean prompted. "And the only girl."

She eyed him warily. She wanted to be careful how much she told him. "That's right."

"I'm surprised your family isn't keeping closer tabs on you."

"Well…my mother has a pretty high-powered position that takes all her time and energy. My three brothers are male versions of her."

"But not you."

"Nope," Zoe admitted. "Which drives them all crazy. I don't understand why since none of them ever has any time for me."

"Do they have any idea where you are?"

"No, but it was my mother's idea for me to…"

"What?"

"See the world. Learn responsibility. Stay out of trouble."

"How is that going for you?" he asked.

"Only time will tell, but it seems to be working out okay."

"I think you're doing great."

"Thanks."

As she rinsed the soap from his hair, Sean closed his eyes. A satisfied smile settled on his lips. He was enjoying his shampoo.

So was she.

A little too much.

Her suggestion to wash his hair had been totally innocent, one more way she could care for him. But touching his hair, his head, was much too intimate.

Zoe felt guilty.

For the shampoo and for not being able to tell him the truth. Sean liked the person he thought she was. So did Zoe.

She gave his head a final rinse to make sure all the shampoo was gone.

Too bad she couldn't leave Zoe Carrington behind and just be Zoe Flynn.

"I guess I should have figured out you are one of those workaholic types."

Sean glanced up from his computer, the one he'd been dying to use for the past week, to find Zoe standing in front of him with a cup of coffee in her hand. "What?"

"You're like a kid playing video games." She set the steaming mug on the end table. "We might have to rethink your allotment of screen time. You're completely obsessed with your computer."

"Not obsessed, just checking e-mail. I've been out of touch with people at the office for a while."

She went into the kitchen. "Whose fault was that?"

"Mine, but it's a busy time. I need to get caught up," Sean explained. "Custom orders are streaming in because of the holidays. We've got a huge PR event coming up at New Year's, the Rail Jam Extravaganza, that could increase our exposure and distribution significantly."

Zoe returned with a cup of coffee for herself. "Is it ever not busy?"

"No, this is pretty typical."

"How do your girlfriends feel about that? When you have one." Her cheeks heated. "A real one, I mean."

"I don't have time for a real girlfriend. Between work, climbing, riding and rescue work, there isn't a lot left over for the women I date."

"You like playing the field."

"Well, yeah," he admitted. "That keeps things casual. I figured out a couple of years ago that no one gets hurt that way."

"So you used to be a heartbreaker."

It wasn't a question. Sean shrugged, uncomfortable with the turn the conversation had taken. "Let's just say I'm careful not to create expectations now."

She sat cross-legged on the floor, cradling her mug in the palms of her hands. "What changed?"

"I grew up."

"But not enough to settle down."

"Ouch."

"Kidding," she joked. "I'm just surprised how focused you've become on work."

"My company is important to me. My employees, too. I owe it to them to make sure everything's running smoothly."

"What do you do when you have a rescue mission to go on or a vacation?" Zoe asked.

"Excuse me?"

"I'm sure this isn't the first time you've been out of the office for an extended amount of time."

"No, it's not," he admitted. "I have a capable staff. Very talented and trustworthy."

"So you should let them do their jobs and take care of things while you recover," she urged. "If they need you, you're only a phone call away."

Zoe made it sound so easy. Maybe it was.

Sean hadn't had this much spare time in eight years. Not since he'd started his snowboarding company at the age of twenty-five. He'd hired the best people he could find and

trained others to do what he wanted. His company had sur-
vived not only rescue missions, but also climbing expedi-
tions to Denali and Patagonia. No doubt, Hughes Snowboards
would survive this.

A part of him wasn't ready to jump back in with both feet.
He liked being with Zoe, playing games and watching television with her. He didn't want to have to give that up completely
just yet.

Sean closed his computer. "I can do that."

Her eyes widened. "Really?"

"Yeah."

A satisfied grin settled on her lips.

"What do you want to do?" he asked.

"That's usually my question."

"Let's shake things up a little," he suggested.

"Let's shake things up a lot."

The mischief gleaming in her eyes filled Sean with hope.
Maybe she was having second thoughts about no more
kissing.

"Why don't we pull out your tree and decorate your house
for Christmas?" she suggested.

Sean never put up a tree until his mother's nagging got to
be too much to bear, but Zoe's excitement made decorating
for Christmastime a little more appealing. "I have decorations, but I don't have a tree to pull out. I cut one down each
year."

She leaned forward. "With an ax like they do in the
movies?"

Smiling, he nodded.

"That must be so much fun to do."

He heard the longing in her voice and remembered how
she'd been humming "It's Beginning to Look a Lot Like
Christmas." Except his house looked as if the holidays were
months away. He felt bad because she was so eager to please
and working so hard, he wanted to return the favor. "Would
you like to cut down a tree for us, Zoe?"

"I'd love to, but I don't know how."

Unfortunately, he wasn't in any shape to go with her. "A good thing I have a few friends who do."

"Got your permit?" Sean asked two days later.

"The tree-cutting permit is right here." Zoe patted her coat pocket. She was dressed, like his friends, in a down jacket, waterproof pants and boots. Only she wore borrowed gear. Still, he couldn't scrub the image of her dancing half-naked in the snow from his mind. "The ten whatever you called them are in the backpack."

"The ten essentials," he said tightly, running through the list in his mind. Map, compass, firestarter, waterproof matches, first-aid kit, knife, flashlight, sunglasses, extra clothing and extra food and water.

Damn, Sean wished he were going with them. He glanced at his legs. Not happening.

Bill Paulson grinned. "So Zoe, did you pack your toothbrush and dental floss, too?"

Lines creased her forehead. "My—?"

"Relax, Zoe. Just some ribbing," Jake explained. "Sean acts like a mother hen whenever we go out on a mission."

Tim Moreno, another OMSAR member and climbing partner who also worked for Hughes Snowboards, nodded. "We have to go over our checklist."

"And review our objective," Bill added.

Jake smiled. "But it is Hughes's job to keep us safe up there."

"And get our sorry asses back down the hill in one piece," Tim added.

"I haven't lost anyone yet." Sean didn't mind poking fun at himself. "At least I haven't lost anyone, except people leaving my team in sheer disgust."

Jake's mouth quirked. "I wonder who that might have been."

"Not now." Even with two useless legs, Sean couldn't help falling into his usual role. He looked at Zoe. "You charged up my cell phone and packed it, right?"

"Dude, Zoe told you. We're set." Jake pulled out a candy bar. "I even brought chocolate."

She laughed. "The eleventh essential."

"You're going to fit right in," Tim said.

She zipped her backpack. "I really appreciate you guys taking me out."

"Even Ebenezer Scrooge needs a Christmas tree," Jake joked.

"Scrooge?" Bill furrowed his brows. "I always thought Hughes was more of a Grinch type."

"Green?" Jake asked.

"Jealous," Bill said with a nod. "Because we get to spend the morning with Zoe."

"Sean's not jealous." A pretty blush colored Zoe's cheeks. "And he's no Scrooge, either. He's the one who suggested I get the tree."

"Sean?" Jake asked.

Tim made a face. "You're kidding."

"I get a small tree every year." Sean's friends continued to stare at him in disbelief. He didn't blame them. "Okay, I do it to appease my mom."

"Your sad excuse for a tree last year made the Charlie Brown Christmas tree look great," Jake joked.

Sean's idea to send Zoe out to cut a nice one down seemed really stupid now. This was totally out of character for him.

"That was last year," he said. "Zoe wanted to decorate the house for Christmas and asked if we could pull out the tree. I discovered she's never cut down a tree before."

She grinned. "It sounds like a lot of fun."

"Well, Zoe," Tim said. "You're in for a treat today. Nothing beats cutting down your own tree."

Jake nodded. "Damn straight."

The doorbell rang.

"I'll get it," she said and walked toward the front door.

"You must really like her to go to all this trouble for a Christmas tree," Tim said.

"Well, you three have to do all the work." Sean lowered his voice. "So here's the deal. Zoe's a city girl. She's not used to being out in the woods. I went over numerous scenarios with her. She knows if she gets separated from you to stay put, but—"

"We're not going to let anything happen to her," Jake said.

Bill nodded. "I'll take extra special care of her for you, dude. I can even short-rope her to me if you like."

Sean eyed him warily. The guy had a reputation with the ladies. "Maybe Leanne should tag along."

"Don't worry, Hughes." Tim nudged his shoulder. "Us married guys will keep the single guy in line. Your girl's safe with us."

Your girl.

That was how Sean was coming to think of Zoe even though nothing physical was going on between them. On second thought, hair washing ranked right up there with back rubs when it came to foreplay. Not that he could even get to second base with Zoe.

Still, the more time he spent with her, the more he liked her. She was always bright, always warm, like the sun on a cold day or a fire in an empty room, even when she was upset and scolding him for overdoing it. He was getting to know her in a way he seldom got to know his here-today-gone-tomorrow dates. He liked the woman he was getting to know. She wasn't just his caregiver. She was a friend. He wished she could be more.

But if he acted on those desires, he risked losing her. Any sort of romantic fling would mess things up. Sean didn't want to do that to her. She needed the job. She needed a place to stay.

The last thing Sean wanted was to hurt her. Once he healed, he wouldn't have time for her anyway.

Better to settle for the quick kisses in front of his family and friends, the card games and surprisingly intimate talks, her smile when she looked at him and her fingers against his scalp when she washed his hair.

The din of conversation and laughter pulled him from his pleasant fantasy of Zoe leaning over him, her chest at eye level.

"Carly and the kids must be here," Jake said.

The familiar sound of paws against hardwood widened Sean's smile. "Denali."

His dog rounded the corner, sliding a little on the floor. Her clear, blue eyes met Sean's. She sprinted toward him, a bundle of energy and excitement.

"Whoa, Denali." Jake grabbed her by the collar before she could pounce on top of Sean. He led her over to the couch as Zoe entered the great room. "Go easy on him, girl."

"Welcome home, baby." Sean patted the couch, and Denali jumped up. She nuzzled and licked his face. He hugged her. "I missed you, too."

"The kids thought you might want to see her. And they wanted to see you." Carly Porter walked in with her ten-year-old niece Kendall and eight-year-old nephew Austin in tow. "Hannah, Garrett and Tyler went Christmas shopping."

"Denali missed you, Sean," Kendall said.

"But we kept her busy so she wouldn't miss you too much," Austin added.

Sean grinned and rubbed the dog. "Thanks."

The two kids were so much like their late father, Nick Bishop. Kendall had his no-fear personality, and Austin looked exactly like him. Nick would be proud of his kids. Sean sure was.

"Denali and I appreciate that." The dog circled then lay against Sean's side. He exchanged a smile with Zoe. "Hey. Did you guys meet Zoe?"

Austin nodded. He looked at her. "Are you one of Sean's models?"

The room went quiet.

"Zoe is a friend of Sean's," Carly said. "I told you that, Austin."

"But Sammy Ross said Sean only dates models," Austin said.

"Sammy Ross says too much," Jake murmured.

"I'm not a model," Zoe answered with an amused smile.

"But she is Sean's girlfriend. That's why she's here taking care of him," Kendall explained as if she knew all the answers. She looked at Zoe. "Mrs. Hughes said once he's better you'll get married. Do you know how many flower girls you're going to have?"

Zoe blushed.

Sean sighed. He would have to have a talk with his mother.

"Let's save the wedding talk for later, Kendall," Carly said to his relief. "They need to get Christmas-tree hunting. And we have lots we want to do with Sean."

"We're going to play video games." Austin jumped from foot to foot. "And build Lego."

"Don't forget baking cookies," Kendall added.

"I can see I'm leaving you in good hands." Zoe pulled her wool beanie over her hair. It reminded him of the first time he'd seen her standing on the side of the road. She walked toward him, and his pulse kicked up a notch. "Have fun."

He would miss her. "You, too."

As Zoe rubbed Denali's head, she leaned over to kiss Sean's cheek.

He didn't want another chaste peck. He didn't want to be dismissed like Denali, with a pat and a treat. He wanted a kiss. Even if it were only for pretend.

At the last second he turned his head. Her lips landed on his. He felt her tense, but she didn't pull her mouth away from him. Instead, she relaxed. He brought his arm around her.

The taste of her, all sweetness and warmth, seeped through Sean, making him feel better than any pain medication could. The best part, however, was that she kissed him back.

Her mouth pressed against his as her lips parted. She arched closer, her jacket crinkling between them until he felt the softness of her chest against him.

Probably for show, but Sean didn't care.

He'd wanted this. Needed this. Needed her.

Denali stood on the couch, stuck her nuzzle between their faces and pushed until Zoe backed away.

"Don't worry, Denali." Zoe laughed with pink cheeks and swollen lips. "I know who the number one girl is around here."

Sean steadied his ragged breathing.

A good thing she knew, because he wasn't so sure anymore. All Sean knew was he wanted to kiss Zoe again. Maybe he should see about getting some mistletoe.

Except...

He wanted more than kisses from Zoe.

Mrs. Hughes said once he's better you'll get married.

Marriage was too extreme, but Sean agreed with his mom on one point. He liked having Zoe around. The only problem was what would happen when he was fully recovered?

How would Zoe fit into his life then? Would she even want to?

Flushed with fresh air and excitement, Zoe entered the great room.

A fire crackled in the river-rock fireplace. Denali lay on her dog pillow with her head resting on a stuffed football toy. Sean sprawled on the couch where she'd last seen him. His long legs rested on the ottoman, his face a study of intense concentration. Kendall and Austin sat on either side of him. All three stared at the video game they played on the large screen television.

The whole scene reminded her of a family sitcom.

Zoe smiled impishly. "Hi, honey, I'm home."

Home. The word struck her with unexpected force.

The governor's mansion had never been like this. She had

lived there since she was eight, but it felt more like a museum than a home. The only time her family sat down together to play games or cards or watch a movie was when the press showed up to do a story on them. Most of the time she'd been on her own.

Zoe barely remembered the large estate, her childhood home, where she'd lived before her mother had been elected. The property had been sold after her father's death.

Denali rose, stretched and lumbered toward her.

Sean glanced over, returning Zoe's smile with one of his own. The sense of homecoming struck again, making her knees go weak.

"Hey, I missed you," he said.

She'd missed him, too. Even though she'd had fun with Jake, Bill and Tim, she'd worried about Sean, wished she could share her experience of cutting down her first Christmas tree with him. But now she was here, she worried even more.

Because this was not her home.

He was not her boyfriend.

And as soon as he was better, she would leave him and Mount Hood behind.

Her smile faded.

"Did you find a tree?" Austin asked.

Zoe cleared her dry throat. "The guys are trying to get it out of the truck."

Sean stood and made his way toward her using the walker. "Trying?"

The kids' aunt, Carly, came out of the bathroom.

"It's a big tree," Zoe admitted.

"This I have to see," Carly said. "Kids, you want to come?"

They were too engrossed in their video game.

Carly shook her head. "I'll be right back."

Sean looked at Zoe with an invitation in his eyes. "You didn't kiss me hello."

Zoe's heart fluttered. "We don't have an audience."

He motioned to the kids totally enraptured by their game.

"I think they count more as chaperones," she said quietly.

Sean grinned and held out his hand. "Did you have fun?"

She let herself take it, noticing how warm and strong his grip was.

"Yes." Zoe focused on being his caretaker, his friend. Anything else wasn't possible. She released his hand. "I only had to use one of my essentials."

"Which one?"

"The chocolate bar."

"Leave it to Porter to remember the most important essential." Sean laughed. "So you found a big tree."

She nodded. "Jake didn't think it would fit your tree stand so he stopped off and bought a bigger one. They're going to put it on outside."

"You better get the beers ready," Sean said.

"What for?"

"Getting a big tree into a stand is at least a two man production. Think lots of choice swear words and grunting."

Zoe was amused. "That sounds awful."

Sean grinned. "Naw. It's tradition."

Zoe arched her brows. "Really? For someone whose friends claim he's a Grinch, I wasn't expecting respect for tradition."

"Traditions are important, Zoe." Kendall said, the video game controller on her lap. "Especially at the holidays. Isn't that right, Sean?"

"That's exactly right," he said.

Austin nodded. "Last year, Sean brought back a Christmas tradition to save him from going stark raving mad at his parents' house and drinking too much and killing one of his cousins."

Zoe looked at Sean. "Oh, really?"

"A cousin twice removed." A sheepish smile crossed his face. "I didn't realize the kids were listening so carefully."

She laughed. "So what is this tradition that saves you from the insane asylum, detox and incarceration?"

Kendall inched forward until she was sitting on the edge of the couch. "Can I tell her, Sean?"

He nodded.

"Before my first daddy died on the mountain, he would take me snowshoeing with a bunch of his friends on Christmas day before dinner. They also used to do it before I was born. And sometimes my mom would go, too."

Zoe had met their mom, Hannah, when she dropped off a pan of lasagna last week. She seemed like a lovely woman with an almost-one-year-old baby boy in addition to Kendall and Austin. Hannah had seemed as devoted to Sean as her children were.

"That sounds like a wonderful tradition." It reaffirmed what Zoe had seen at the hospital, how much Sean was a part of the community here in Hood Hamlet. He not only attracted friends, but also knew how to keep them. She'd tried, but hadn't been able to sustain relationships that way.

"It's my favorite tradition," Sean admitted.

"What about opening presents from Santa?" Austin asked.

"Much better than presents," Sean answered.

Zoe remembered all the bouquets from women in the hospital. He'd admitted to only dating casually. Maybe Sean didn't sustain all relationships. Only friendships.

"Everyone waited six years until Aunt Carly came back to Hood Hamlet last Christmas to go snowshoeing again," Kendall added.

"We got to go with them," Austin said. "They gave us snowshoes. We had hot chocolate and cookies, too. It was awesome."

"Sounds like a wonderful tradition," Zoe said.

Kendall nodded. "I can't wait to go again."

As Austin stared at Sean's legs, the smile on the boy's face turned upside down. "Are you going to be better by Christmas?"

MELISSA McCLONE 121

"No, little dude." Sean messed up Austin's mop of blond hair. "I'm going to have to sit this year out."

"But you have to be there." Austin stuck his jaw out. "Please."

"Oh, please, Sean." Kendall's eyes gleamed. "It won't be the same if you're not there. And Denali, too."

Zoe's heart ached for all of them. She fought the urge to reach out to Sean.

He gripped the walker. "If there was any way, you know I would be there."

"Maybe we can figure out something," Zoe offered.

"Yes!" the kids said in unison.

As they gave each other high fives, Sean motioned to his legs.

Zoe shrugged. "Christmas is still a couple weeks away."

"My mom says Christmas is a time of magic and miracles, especially on the mountain," Kendall said.

Zoe smiled at her. "Your mom is right."

Sean shook his head. At least he didn't say bah humbug.

"Ho, ho, ho," a male voice bellowed from the front door. "Christmas tree delivery for Mr. Hughes."

Jake, Tim and Paul entered wearing Santa hats and carrying in the Christmas tree. Carly followed with an old-fashioned red cap with white lace, the kind Mrs. Claus might wear, on her head.

Austin squealed with laughter. Kendall giggled.

The scent of pine filled the air. Denali ran to sniff the tree.

Sean whistled. "That is a big tree."

"Size matters, Hughes," Bill joked.

"Want to put my tree up next to yours?" Sean asked.

"I've seen your tree, Paulson," Tim said. "Better cut your losses now."

"I still can't believe you got that tree in the truck," Carly said. "Is it going to fit in here?"

Jake held the end with the tree stand attached. "Have a little faith in the magic of Christmas, beautiful."

"The tree looked so small compared to the others towering around it." When Zoe had seen how big it was in comparison to the truck, her heart had dropped to her feet. "But it will fit."

Please. She prayed for a little Christmas magic. Let the tree fit.

Tim and Bill righted the tree while Jake held the stand.

"It fits," Bill announced.

Zoe breathed a sigh of relief. "Told you so."

"You did." Sean smiled. "But I think we're going to need a lot more lights and ornaments than I have."

Carly leaned against her husband Jake and smiled. "It's lovely as it is."

"Beautiful," Kendall agreed.

"Perfect." Sean looked at Zoe, a smile still on his face. "You did good, babe."

She glowed at his praise.

This might not be her home, but this would be the only Christmas she ever spent in Hood Hamlet with Sean. Zoe was going to make it a Christmas to remember. She wanted to make sure Sean never forgot it.

Or her.

CHAPTER EIGHT

THE NEXT day ZOE crawled under the branches of the Christmas tree to check the water level in the tree stand. Almost empty. She tipped the pitcher awkwardly to refill it. "I never had to do this at my mother's. I can't believe how much water this tree needs."

"Cut trees drink a lot at first." Sean sat with his legs on the ottoman and a MacBook Pro on his lap. He'd been working a little each day in addition to his physical therapy and workout sessions in his garage gym. "But in a couple of weeks, it won't need much at all."

She wiggled out on her stomach and sat back on her heels to grin at him. "Sounds like you. Lots of care to start, and now look at you."

"Gee thanks," he said dryly. "I always wanted to be compared to a Christmas tree."

"Hey, I love this tree." Realizing what she'd just said, she blushed. "Because it's fresh. I mean…its size. Er, shape. The way it smells."

"It's a great tree," Sean said, rescuing her from embarrassment. "Better than the small one I had last year. It's only going to be tall trees from now on."

He meant next year, in the future.

Zoe's stomach clenched. She'd never given much thought to the future. That had always bothered her family, but now she couldn't stop the questions swirling in her mind.

Where would she be in twelve months? What would she be doing? Who would she be with?

She rose and returned the water pitcher to the kitchen. "Well, you wouldn't want Bill to have the biggest tree, would you?"

Sean laughed. "Are you ready to decorate?"

"Let's wait until you're on crutches and can help."

"You don't have to."

"I want to wait." Her gaze drifted from the tree to him. "The only trees I've decorated were little dinky tabletop jobs, and I had to do it myself. I want this tree to be different."

"Your family never had a big tree?"

The trees in the governor's mansion were always huge, but... "My mom likes themed trees so every year she hires a decorator."

"That must cost a pretty penny."

Nodding, Zoe thought about the different trees through the years. The bird one with turtle doves, French hens, calling birds and partridges had been her favorite. "My mother loves showing off her Christmas tree. No expense is spared."

"Everybody has their own priorities."

"Her trees are always gorgeous, but it's not much fun watching the decorator's crew put on the ornaments instead of getting to do it ourselves."

"You never got to decorate your family's tree?"

"Never," Zoe admitted. "Sad, isn't it?"

She tried to sound lighthearted, but failed.

"Let's wait then so we can decorate the tree together," Sean said. "We need to get more stuff anyway. Why don't you see what decorations are in the container so we know what to buy?"

Zoe carried the large green-and-red container that Hank had brought in this morning from the entryway to the great room. She placed it near the tree. "At least you have some things."

"Most were given to me, including the box," Sean admitted. "Christmas decorations aren't something guys put a lot of thought into. At least this guy."

"I'll Be Home For Christmas" played on the radio. As Zoe hummed along, she removed the lid from the container. She really did feel at home here with Sean.

A green-and-red tree skirt sat on top. Each triangular piece was made from a different fabric pattern. Stripes, plaids, gingham. Nothing too feminine, yet the feel wasn't too masculine, either. Perfect for a family.

Zoe's insides twisted. "This is nice."

"Aunt Vera made it for me," he said. "There are matching stockings."

Zoe placed the tree skirt on the container's lid. "The stockings are right here."

She held three quilted stockings in the air to see how they would hang. They were pieced together with the same fabrics used on the tree skirt. Sean's name was embroidered on the white cuff of one of the stockings. A smaller stocking had Denali's name stitched on it. "Who's the blank stocking for?"

Sean rolled his eyes. "It's Aunt Vera's not-so-subtle hint I should settle down."

"You weren't kidding when you said they were on your back about getting married."

"Nope. I should have never adopted a dog or built this house. Both gave my family the wrong idea."

"A four-bedroom house isn't your typical bachelor pad. It might give women the wrong idea, too."

"I'm upfront with the women I date. They know I don't have that kind of time to put into a relationship."

"That must go over well," she teased, but a part of her knew how those women must feel. His words reminded Zoe of her family. Work had always taken priority for them. And that had left her feeling like an outsider and alone.

"Not always, but they need to understand I have a lot going on. Normally, that is. When I'm not injured."

Zoe glanced at the tree and thought of how things would

be in a couple weeks. Sean would probably be in the office every day and working out when he wasn't. A big change from now. "Maybe if you meet the right woman someday, you'll want to make time for a relationship."

"Maybe." His tone suggested that was unlikely. "In the meantime, you can use the stocking."

She flushed. His Aunt Vera had made the blank stocking for his future wife, not his pretend girlfriend.

"I don't need a stocking." Zoe carefully placed the stockings on top of the tree skirt. "I haven't had one in years."

"You have to have one here."

"Why is that?"

"Stockings, especially handmade ones, are a Hughes family tradition," he explained. "Besides, if you don't have a stocking where will Santa put your presents?"

Zoe imagined her name embroidered on the blank stocking. She pushed the thought from her mind. "Don't you mean my lump of coal?"

"Nah, you've been a very good girl." He raised a brow. "But we still have a little time until Christmas Eve. If you want some help doing something naughty, I'm happy to oblige."

His words loosened the tight feeling in her chest. She wished he could oblige her.

No, Zoe reminded herself, she didn't.

She pulled out a box of a single strand of lights. "White lights?"

"I bought those myself," he said. "I grew up with multicolored lights, but the white ones look like stars to me."

Her heart melted. "I can't believe your friends think you're the Grinch."

"I don't mind. I have an image to uphold." Sean struck a pose. "Gruff loner with a dog."

"Don't you mean overprotective mother hen?" she teased.

"I'll ignore that."

She pulled out a box filled with a dozen colored balls. Next came three silver stocking holders that spelled JOY, no doubt gifts based on the number. Finally she removed a large shoebox. "What's in here?"

"All the ornaments my cousins' kids and friends' kids have made me over the years."

Zoe opened the lid to find everything from paper ornaments scribbled with crayons to painted wood ones. "These are adorable. Maybe we could invite all your cousins' kids over to make more ornaments for the tree."

"If you do that, everyone is going to want to come."

"The more the merrier. We could make it a tree-trimming party." Excitement rippled through her. "I've always wanted to string popcorn and cranberries and make a garland."

Sean didn't say anything.

And then Zoe remembered with a pang. "You don't like family get-togethers."

"I didn't like family get-togethers when my family was breathing down my neck telling me to settle down," he admitted. "Now that I have you, it's not a problem."

"But..."

He smiled at her. "You said you wanted this tree to be different. Let's have a party."

Zoe jumped up, ran to the couch and sat next to him. "We'll need to call an event planner right away. Is there someone you normally use?"

"Event planner? Honey, this is a tree-trimming party in Hood Hamlet, not a wedding in... Where did you say you were from?"

Oops. No way could she tell him her hometown. "I most recently lived in L.A. I'll just call a caterer instead."

"Uh-uh. Try a potluck."

"Really?" she asked.

He nodded. "My family likes to cook. They expect to be asked to bring food to a party. Especially a family gathering."

She'd never been to a potluck in her life. "Well, I don't want to step on any of the Hughes's toes."

"One phone call to my mother, and your work will be done."

Zoe smiled uncertainly. Organizing a family gathering was not at all the sort of thing her mother would enjoy.

Sean eyed her. "What kind of parties are you used to, Zoe?"

"Not that different from yours," she hedged. "It's just we don't have an event planner in the family."

He raised an eyebrow.

"Your mother," Zoe explained. Now that she thought about it, about being surrounded by family, even borrowed family, for the holidays, her spirits soared.

He studied her. "Happy?"

"Very." She hugged him. "Thank you."

His arms circled around her. "You're welcome."

It was just a hug, a gesture between friends, but his warmth and closeness sent her pulse racing. She didn't want to let go. Sean didn't seem in any hurry to end their hug, either.

Zoe looked up at him, her face mere inches away.

He gazed down at her, his eyes full of desire.

She swallowed and glanced at his lips. It would be so easy to kiss him. All she had to do was lift her chin and move her head...

"Naughty?" he inquired huskily, his pupils dilated. "Or nice?"

Her heart leapt. Zoe struggled to breathe.

Naughty.

But if she kissed Sean and things went sour, she risked ruining everything she'd been working so hard to do and be. She wouldn't be able to stay here and care for him. She wouldn't be able to show her mother she'd learned to be responsible.

That wouldn't be nice at all.

Keep it light, Zoe told herself.

"I think we'd better both be good," she said. "I don't want either of us to wake up with..."

"Coal in our stockings?"

Zoe shook her head. "Regrets."

No regrets this morning. Last night on the couch with Zoe had been another story, but he'd gone along with Zoe's wishes again.

Sean made his way out of the orthopedic surgeon's office on crutches. He respected Zoe's decision to keep things all business while he was laid up. But his sutures had been removed. He no longer needed the air cast on his ankle or the stupid walker.

He was feeling stronger, more himself, more confident.

Sean didn't want to drive Zoe away, but it was time to test the limits.

"Let's grab some lunch." He wanted her to see him as a man, not a patient. "Then swing by my office."

The look of concern he'd gotten to know so well over the past two weeks filled Zoe's eyes. "Are you sure you're up for all that? You're taking some awfully big steps right now."

"I'll take smaller ones." Just like the small steps he wanted to take with her. Sean breathed in the crisp, cold air. "I'm up for it."

Zoe unlocked and opened the passenger door of his truck for him. "As long as you don't overdo it."

Sean slid in and stuck the crutches behind him. "Me, overdo it?"

"Overdo is your middle name."

He wouldn't mind being over her. Doing her, either. The little fantasy made him smirk. "I can't keep sitting around and doing nothing. It's totally against my nature."

"I know." She walked around the back of the truck and climbed into the driver's seat. "Why do you think I have to watch you practically 24/7?"

"My devastatingly good looks and charm?"

She turned the key in the ignition. The engine roared to life. "Sorry, but as your caretaker I'm immune to those things."

Zoe hadn't seemed so last night. In fact, she'd looked almost feverish when she gazed into his eyes. Just thinking about it raised his temperature. "Better be careful, oh caretaker of mine, I'm always up for a challenge."

Zoe sat at a small table across from Sean at a quaint little café. Celtic harp music played from hidden speakers. A server, clad in black, removed their plates and silverware.

It was the kind of place she liked to eat at, good atmosphere, delicious food, but hadn't had the chance to since striking out on her own with a monthly allowance to budget.

She raised her glass of strawberry lemonade and smiled. "Here's to you getting such a positive report from your doctor."

Sean lifted his glass of soda and clinked it against hers. "And getting rid of the stupid walker."

Zoe took a sip. "I'm happy your recovery is going so well."

"I'm getting better."

"You are." The realization made her happy, but a little sad that her usefulness and time with Sean had a definite end now. With his legs under the table and his crutches propped against the wall, he didn't look injured or like her patient at all. He looked whole and virile and tempting. Uh-oh. "Thanks for suggesting we stop for lunch."

"You're welcome." Sean slid cash into the leather folder and handed her one of the chocolate mints wrapped in green foil. "It's about time we had a first date."

She choked on her lemonade. "We're not dating."

"My family doesn't know that. If anyone asks what our first date was, we can tell them this place."

"Couldn't we just tell them we met at Timberline?"

"That wasn't a date. I didn't pay for your lift ticket."

He was teasing her. She was tempted to play along. Part of her wanted the fantasy that this was a date. A real one.

But Zoe knew better. Even if things were different, Sean Hughes didn't have the time to make a relationship work.

He'd said so himself. She was tired of being someone's afterthought. She didn't want to do that again.

She took another sip of her drink. The strawberry lemonade tasted bittersweet. "I didn't realize pretend relationships had dating rules."

"They follow regular dating rules, which reminds me—" Sean raised her hand to his mouth and kissed it "—official dates should include a kiss."

Zoe's hand tingled at the spot his lips had touched her skin. "Shouldn't you have to walk me to the door?"

"That's a given. We live together."

The way he said "together" sent a ball of heat zipping through her.

Not good.

She sipped her ice water. "So what's next?"

"How does taking my pretend girlfriend to work sound?"

"What if your real-life caretaker thinks you should go home instead?"

"I'd tell her I feel great," he said. "If that didn't work I'd remind her I'm the boss and the doctor said it was okay."

"Guess we're going to work, then."

Zoe was curious, interested to see the man, not the patient she'd been spending time with. Maybe what she learned about Sean would make her struggle to be responsible easier to handle.

She parked the truck at Hughes Snowboards and slid out. By the time she'd reached the back, Sean was waiting for her.

"You're fast on the crutches," she said.

He negotiated his way through the gray slush in the parking lot. "I've had some practice using them before."

Worry had her biting her lip. "I guess you've had a lot of injuries as a rescue worker."

"I've never been injured on a mission," he explained. "Rescuer safety is our number one priority."

"Then how did you get hurt?"

"I climb for fun and ride as much as I can. I'm careful, but stuff happens."

"Like equipment breaking."

"Or rock fall and a hundred other things." He winked at her. "Good thing I'm a fast healer."

"Yeah. A fast healer." Zoe tried to muster some enthusiasm, but failed miserably. The bad news kept coming. She'd thought Sean might need her help into January. Now she wondered if he'd need her past Christmas. As she followed him into the factory, she dragged her feet. "That's a very good thing."

Over the noise of machines and the buzz of fans, music blared from speakers. Snowboarding posters covered the walls along with brightly colored banners with Hughes, Catch Some Air and Ride printed on them. She recognized a couple of people who had visited Sean at the hospital and at home.

Sean waved at one employee. Another hugged him. Everyone looked happy to see him back. He smiled, looking alert and confident and in complete control, as if he hadn't spent the past two weeks sitting on the couch playing games, reading and watching television.

"This place is big," she said.

"Burton has nothing to worry about from us." Sean stopped to check a board being built. "We have a niche market, but we're seeing steady growth in a couple of sectors. We're adding new product lines and expanding old ones."

Sean had always come across as intelligent. They'd had long talks about politics, economics and a whole bunch of other subjects, but today he seemed so different.

This was one of the first days she'd seen him in clothing other than shorts and T-shirts. Aunt Vera had modified a pair of khaki pants for him to wear over his encased left leg. The colors in his long-sleeved shirt brought out the green in his hazel eyes. But the differences she saw went deeper than his apparel.

He wasn't Hank and Connie's son or a mountain rescue volunteer. Sean was a businessman, a successful one given the size of his factory and the number of employees who worked for him.

She was impressed and intimidated. "You love what you do."

"Best job in the world." He thought for a moment. "Except when the prototype binding I designed broke on Thanksgiving Day. That pretty much sucked."

"I know how that hurt you personally, but I didn't even think about how it could impact your business."

"Business is fine," Sean reassured her. "I've also gotten to spend time with you. So the accident wasn't all bad."

Zoe's pulse skittered.

His acceptance of what had happened and his reassurance to her was so different from her family's reaction whenever something went wrong. They would point fingers and assign blame. No one ever saw the silver lining like Sean.

Her respect for him grew.

"Let me show you the other building," he said.

Zoe heard the pride in his voice. Despite her worries he might be overdoing it, she wanted to see more of this side of him.

They exited the factory via thick double doors, crossed beneath a covered walkway and into another building, one that looked newer. She noticed the quiet right away. No music or machines. Poster-size snowboarding photographs lined the walls. Cubicle walls filled the open space with three offices along the side wall.

"We have a retail shop in Hood Hamlet that Tim runs," Sean said. "Everything else is sold on the Internet or by distributors."

"Argh! I hate pink," a male voice said. "Why don't they just buy Roxy or some other chick brand?"

"Excuse me," Sean said and made his way toward a cubicle near the back. Zoe followed.

Energy drink cans and candy bar wrappers littered a desk. A twentysomething guy with shoulder-length brown hair stared at a computer monitor. He looked totally dejected.

"What's up, Taylor?" Sean asked.

"This custom top sheet, dude." Taylor pointed to the monitor and a sorry-looking snowboard that resembled the color of medicine used to calm an upset stomach. "Customer wants something 'unique' for his seven-year-old daughter. She likes pink and princesses."

"Let's see what you've got." Sean stared at the monitor. "Okay, you've got the pink covered. The swirl of stars is a nice touch, but it doesn't say princess yet. Try to think like a seven-year-old girl."

Taylor groaned. "Dude, this is just wrong. It's like drawing with my own blood. It's killing me."

Zoe covered her mouth to hide her smile.

"Come on, kid," Sean encouraged. "You're my best graphic designer."

"I'm your only one since Cocoa left for Vermont."

"You can do it." Sean patted Taylor's shoulder. "The little girl riding this board could be a future gold medalist. Let that inspire you."

Taylor gave him a look. "Princesses don't shred, man."

Zoe pressed her lips together to keep from laughing. Poor Taylor. No doubt this was a galaxy—make that a fairy-tale kingdom—away from his comfort level. "Could I make a suggestion?"

Both Sean and Taylor looked her way.

Sean motioned her into the cubicle. "Taylor, this is Zoe. She knows more about princesses and the color pink than either of us could ever hope to."

"Do you have a piece of scratch paper?" she asked.

Taylor shoved white paper and a pen into her hands. "If you can save me from this misery, the first round of drinks is on me."

"Let's see if this helps." Zoe thought back to one of her favorite art classes from college. She sketched Taylor's basic star design and added in some wands, crowns, glass slippers and flourishes that matched the way he'd drawn the stars. She saw a set of colored pencils on the desk. Her fingers itched. "If I had more time…"

"Take all the time you want. Whatever you need," Taylor said.

Zoe opened the metal case of pencils and pulled out three different shades of pinks. With rapid strokes, she feathered in the design using all three colors, explaining as she drew. "Try starting with a softer pink. Overlay darker shades so you get a mix. That will add some texture, too. See?"

She showed them her drawing.

"Dude, that's totally rad." Taylor stared at the drawing. "I mean, Zoe. Thanks."

Sean stared at her with gratitude in his eyes. "Yeah, thanks."

"You're both welcome."

"Everything cool now?" Sean asked his designer.

Taylor's nod was barely perceptible. He was too busy working.

She followed Sean out of the cubicle.

"Do you have a background in design or does it come naturally?" he asked.

"I have a degree in fashion design, but no job experience," she said. "My family thought my major was a huge waste of time and effort, but I love working with shape and color. I figured since they'd eventually force me to attend graduate school for business or law, I could afford to indulge myself as an undergrad."

"I can't believe they didn't recognize your talent."

His words sent her confidence soaring. "My mother thought my designs were cute doodles."

"Unbelievable," Sean said. "The Christmas tree, the top sheet. You've got an incredible eye. You're good at what you do, Zoe."

"Thanks." Inside her suede boots, she wiggled her toes. "That's the nicest thing anyone has ever said to me."

"You've been hanging with the wrong crowd, then."

She stared up at him. "You might be right."

"You should think about using your degree."

The idea of working in design had never crossed Zoe's mind. She'd always believed her brothers had been right about her degree being worthless in the real world, the business world they inhabited. "Maybe I will once you're better and it's time for me to…"

"There's no reason for you to think about finding another job right now," Sean said.

She hadn't been thinking about a job. She'd been thinking about having to leave.

"I still need you," he continued.

Good. She liked him needing her. And until this moment she hadn't a clue what she might do once he no longer did. Getting a job couldn't be that hard. After all the fashion shows and benefits she'd attended over the years, she had contacts in the industry. Her notoriety might even come in handy for once.

Zoe glanced at Sean.

But finding a job would mean leaving Hood Hamlet, most likely Oregon. She didn't want to think about leaving right now. Not until after Christmas. Maybe not at all.

On Saturday, Sean couldn't believe this was his house.

"Jingle Bell Rock" played on his stereo. The scents of spiced apple cider lingered in the air. A buffet of finger foods and desserts lined the kitchen island.

Zoe supervised a bunch of kids making ornaments at the dining table. She was laughing and encouraging them, glue on her fingers and glitter in her hair. Sean smiled. She looked like his own personal Christmas angel.

Outside, his dad, uncles and cousins hung Christmas lights on the front of Sean's house and his back deck. But today, Sean didn't even mind being stuck inside. Today he could touch and kiss Zoe all he wanted. For his family's sake, even though it was really for his own.

Connie put her arm around Sean and gave him a squeeze. "I'm so happy Zoe and you wanted to do this."

"It was mainly her, Mom."

"But you could have said no." His mother gave him another hug. "Thank goodness you didn't listen to us going on about settling down. I'm glad you waited for Zoe. The two of you are good together."

Sean took a sip of eggnog. He'd been hearing that a lot today from his family. Aunt Vera had danced an actual jig when she saw the three stockings hanging on the fireplace.

Normally, his family's interference drove him up the wall. Yet today he didn't mind so much. Maybe it was the eggnog. Maybe, whispered a little voice in the back of his mind, it was Zoe. "She's a great girl," Sean said.

"Don't forget about your grandmother's ring in the safe-deposit box."

"Mom." He didn't really mind their interference. Not when their presence in his house made it possible for him to get his hands on Zoe. But they were still playing roles, he realized, with his family and with each other. He was getting tired of it.

"Just a friendly reminder." Connie's smile widened. "I'm not trying to push you into anything. That seems to be happening all on its own."

Sean couldn't disagree with her about that. He and Zoe were getting closer. Granted, they spent most of their waking hours together. Attraction simmered, yet they continued to only exchange chaste kisses and hugs. Mostly for show. Unfortunately.

"Oh, boy," Connie said. "Aunt Vera has a sprig of mistletoe and she's headed Zoe's way. You better get over there before someone else gets a kiss."

No one was going to kiss his girl. Sean gripped the handles on his crutches. "On my way, Mom."

"Oh, Rebecca." Zoe stared at the wood ornament covered in gold, red and pink glitter. "What a pretty star. I love it."

Rebecca, the six-year-old daughter of Mary Sue and Will Townsend, beamed. "It's for you, Zoe."

"Thank you." Zoe hugged Rebecca, the epitome of sugar and spice and everything nice. "Do you want to hang it on the tree?"

The little girl's brunette ponytail bobbed as she nodded. "I'll be right back."

"Here comes the mistletoe," Aunt Vera said in a singsong voice. "Who's going to get a kiss?"

Two young boys grimaced, as if kissing were the yuckiest thing that could happen. A couple of girls raised their hands, wanting to be picked.

Aunt Vera stopped behind her. "It looks like...Zoe."

Zoe looked up to see mistletoe hanging over her head. "Who shall I kiss?"

"It better be me or there will be blood," Sean said.

Anticipation quickly replaced the amusement in his eyes. Zoe knew exactly how he felt. She wet her lips.

"Stand up, girlie," Aunt Vera said. "The boy's on crutches."

Zoe rose.

Sean stood with his crutches pressed up near his armpits and held out his arms to her.

She went to him, knowing everyone was looking at them.

He'd made no secret of wanting her, but as long as she pretended to Sean and to herself kissing was for show, it wouldn't have to lead anywhere. As long as they had an audience, kissing him was safe.

Sean's mouth captured hers without a moment's hesitation. His lips moved with a tenderness that made her ache. Once again, he made her feel cherished, special, desired.

The taste of him made her drunk, as if someone had spiked the cider.

His arms circled Zoe. He pulled her closer.

She went eagerly, pressing against his strong, hard chest.

The kiss heated up. His tongue tasted, explored her mouth. She was awash in sensation. She struggled to remain in control, knowing people, children, could see them.

It wasn't easy.

Days, okay, weeks, of pent-up longing poured out and went into her kiss. Zoe's hands splayed his back. She could feel the muscular ridges beneath his shirt.

Her pulse raced. Her blood boiled. She didn't want to stop kissing him.

"Get a room," one of his cousins yelled.

The kiss came to an abrupt end. Zoe backed away from Sean at the same time he backed away from her.

Embarrassed by getting so carried away, Zoe stared at the floor. She could only imagine how she looked. She felt hot, as if someone had cranked the thermostat. Her lips felt bruised, swollen, tingly.

Her gaze met Sean's. The desire in his eyes sent her already-racing pulse skittering. He wanted to kiss her again. Good, because she wanted to kiss him again, too. And again. And again. And...

A sudden chill shivered down her spine. Her breath stilled in her chest. She couldn't pretend anymore, to Sean or to herself.

His family had returned to what they were doing. Decorating, hanging ornaments, eating. Soon they would leave. She and Sean would be alone.

Alone.

Free to do whatever they wanted to.

For real.

That made her realize how dangerous it was to be living alone with him. To her heart and to her mother's campaign.

"I'll have to leave the mistletoe here," Aunt Vera quipped.

Two of Sean's cousins nudged each other.

Zoe forced a smile. She glanced at the newspapers covering the table where the kids painted and glued. She could imagine the tabloid headlines if they found out she was living with Sean, not as his caretaker, but as his...

She couldn't bring herself to say it.

Staring deeply into her eyes, Sean tucked a strand of hair behind her ear.

Her heart went pitter-pat.

"We'll pick this up later," he whispered.

Oh, no. Her pulse pounded in her ears. Neither one of them was pretending now, but how could she admit the truth?

Zoe Flynn Carrington, party girl, wild child, governor's exiled daughter, was falling in love.

And she didn't know what to do about it.

But with her mother's special election and ultimatum hanging over her, Zoe couldn't let her impulses or her hormones plunge her into another scandal. No matter how she felt about Sean.

CHAPTER NINE

SEAN waved goodbye to his parents, the last ones to leave the party. He closed and locked the front door. Now he and Zoe wouldn't be disturbed if someone had forgotten something.

The mind-blowing kiss from this afternoon had been on his mind for hours. If not for his cousin's heckling, Sean would have kept kissing Zoe. He'd completely forgotten about their audience. He'd forgotten everything except her. He wanted to feel that way again. "I finally have you all to myself."

Zoe retreated into the kitchen. He followed her.

He'd been trying not to push Zoe into anything. He'd been good, patient, nice. Now it was time to be...naughty.

Sean grinned.

She picked up a serving spoon from the drying rack on the counter and placed it in the drawer. "I need to make sure everything's cleaned up."

He appreciated her work ethic. She made sure she earned every single dollar he paid her. He respected that. Her. But even the most stellar employee needed a...break.

Sean made his way toward her, not letting the crutches get in the way. He knew what he wanted tonight. "Later."

Her smile wavered. She looked uncomfortable. Nervous. "Don't want to wake up to a mess."

"Zoe, I'm done playing games. I want you."

He'd upped the ante. Finally said what had been on his mind for weeks. Hell, from the first day he'd met her. Now all he could do was stand and wait.

Would she check, call, raise or fold?

Zoe's brows furrowed, as if she were mulling his words over in her mind and trying to make a decision.

"I don't want to play games. I'm tired of pretending." Sean leaned against the counter. "Let's make something real out of this thing between us."

She picked up a silver cookie sheet and held it in front of her like a shield. "You need me."

"Damn straight, I need you," he admitted. "Come here."

Her cheeks turned a bright pink. "I meant you still need me to take care of you."

Not this again. He moved toward her. "Stop bluffing and pretending. We both know that kiss today wasn't for show. There's something very real going on here. It's time to take things to the next level."

Zoe clutched the edges of the cookie sheet until her knuckles turned white. "I wish I could."

"There's nothing stopping us."

"I'm stopping it," she said. "My role here is getting a little blurry. I like you, Sean. I can't believe how much I like you. But I can't accept a salary, live in your house and have a romantic relationship with you at the same time."

"Why not?"

"It's like you're paying me to…be here."

He was insulted she'd think that way about him. About them. About herself. "Is this you talking or your mother?"

A beat passed. And another. "Both of us, I think. I want to be responsible."

"Don't you think you're being overly cautious?"

"Better overly cautious than too impulsive."

He took a deep breath. "Okay. I hear you. But we're both adults. We can handle this."

She didn't look convinced. "For how long? You won't need my help much longer."

"Zoe, even after I'm one hundred percent recovered, I still want you around."

"That's nice to hear." Despite the warmth in her eyes, tense lines still marred her forehead and bracketed her face. "But...I remember what you said about dating casually. How long do your relationships usually last?"

Her question caught him off guard. "The past doesn't matter."

"Please, Sean."

"You can't judge our relationship by how I felt, or didn't feel, about someone in the past. You're different, Zoe. You're special."

"Are you sure about that?"

The vulnerability he saw in her eyes was like a vise gripping his heart.

"Yes," Sean said gently. He hadn't had a relationship with a woman that wasn't purely physical in years. "Usually I meet someone, we see each other a few times, and it's over. I've never spent time getting to know someone the way I've gotten to know you these past weeks."

"You said you didn't have time for a relationship."

"I'll make time for you."

"I want to believe that."

"Then believe it."

"It's not just you," Zoe admitted. "I've made a lot of mistakes in the past."

"It doesn't matter what happened before I met you."

She gazed into his eyes, as if she wanted to believe that, too. "This is the first time I haven't plunged headfirst into a relationship myself. It's been...nice."

"Frustrating."

"That, too." She smiled up at him. "I really like you, but I need to do this right."

"Be responsible."

"Yes," she said. "Could we wait a little longer until I'm no longer your official caretaker? Maybe I could find a job around here. A place to stay."

He'd hire her in an instant as a graphic designer. But that would only add another complication. He couldn't date an employee.

Her words nagged at him.

It's like you're paying me to...be here.

Zoe was right. He didn't want to put her in an awkward position. He would have to wait. Or he'd have to think of something else. Make some calls. Make an effort. Leanne had mentioned something about getting a roommate. "I'll do whatever it takes, Zoe."

"Thank you."

Sean caressed her cheek. Truth was he couldn't care less if she found a job or another place to stay. He was willing to give her what she seemed to need: a home, a big family and financial security. Those things were nothing compared to what she gave him. "I'm the one who should be thanking you."

She smiled up at him.

His breath hitched.

"But let's get one thing straight," Sean said. "You're not my pretend girlfriend. You're my real one. And I still plan on kissing you when we're with my family."

Her eyes widened. "You don't see your family all that much."

"Not usually, but don't forget—" he grinned "—it's Christmastime. You said it yourself, holidays are a time for family."

Retail therapy had always lifted Zoe's spirits. She enjoyed the noise, the energy, the glittering mall decorations. Still, she worried about Sean's ability to navigate the jostling Christmas crowd.

"Are you sure this was a good idea?" She glanced at Sean, walking on his crutches next to her. "I can't believe you wanted to come shopping."

He shrugged. "Everybody shops at Christmas. Besides, we needed to get out of the house."

Because of the limits she'd set on their relationship.

Not that Sean wasn't cooperating. They still enjoyed each other's company, the poker and video games, the discussions of work and family and even the weather. But as much as Zoe tried to keep things the same, there had been a shift in their relationship since the tree-trimming party and that kiss. The lack of physical contact was beginning to feel as false as their original ruse.

Sean Hughes was everything she could ask for in a boyfriend. Smart, funny, caring and giving. Strong, responsible, courageous, too. He didn't care if she could cook or made mistakes. He liked her for who she was or who he thought she was. She couldn't wait to take things to the next level.

As soon as Sean's leg was healed.

As soon as she told him the truth.

Her heart beat faster.

No. Zoe couldn't tell him the truth now. She didn't want anything to spoil Christmas.

Four singers, dressed in old-fashioned Victorian costumes, sang Christmas carols underneath a thirty-foot lit tree decorated with twinkling lights and big metallic ornaments.

She stared up at it, thinking of their tree at home. "This is all so bright and pretty."

"Very pretty," he said, looking at her. "Do you know what you want Santa to bring you?"

"I've already gotten what I wanted." Zoe smiled at him. "I get to spend a white Christmas in the mountains with you and your family. That's the best present ever."

"What about spending Christmas with your own family?" His eyes were warm, his tone suddenly serious. "Wouldn't you rather be with them?"

Her stomach knotted. She was touched by his concern. Panicked by it, too.

"It's not practical this year." Not possible, even if she wanted to be with them. She would have more fun here with him and his family. "Really, it's better I'm in Hood Hamlet. Trust me."

"Are you sure?" he asked.

"Yes," she said firmly. "I plan on calling my mother on Christmas."

"Do they have my address?" Sean asked. "To send your presents to?"

"No, but my family's not big on gifts," she explained. "They usually give gift cards or cash. That sort of thing."

"Unlike my family who are very big on gifts," he said ruefully. "I've got a huge list. We'd better get started."

Zoe noticed the crowd, the people carrying packages and shopping bags. She knew Sean well enough to know he would never complain or ask to leave. Not until they'd accomplished the—what had Bill called it?—objective. "What if you hang out in one place and be the keeper of the gift list? I can buy the items and bring them back here for you to approve and check off. That way you don't have to worry about walking around on your crutches and I don't have to carry everything at the same time."

Sean glanced around. "That sounds like a plan. It's more crowded than I thought it would be."

"Christmas is less than a week away." Zoe motioned to an empty table, pleased she could help him this way. She liked taking care of him, liked knowing she was needed. "Sit there. I'll get you a cup of coffee then hit the stores. We'll be out of here before you need a refill."

He sat. "Spoken like a true shopping expert."

The words sent a chill down Zoe's spine. She handed him his list.

When Sean finally learned who she really was, he would realize how close his words were to the truth. He would find out a lot more things about her, her family and her reputation. She hoped he wouldn't be too upset.

Swallowing a sigh, Zoe gave him a pen. "Be right back."

While Zoe shopped, Sean used his iPhone to buy her Christmas present.

It's not practical this year.

Maybe not. But maybe it wasn't practical because she couldn't afford to go home. No permanent address. No money for Thanksgiving dinner. No way to get back to her family if she wanted to.

He could fix that.

Sean knew exactly what to give Zoe—a plane ticket, an airline voucher actually, so she could visit her family when she wanted to. His finger hovered over the order button.

Sean worried she would think he was interfering.

Hell, he was interfering.

With good intentions, of course.

Just like his family always interfered with him.

The realization made him wince. But the thought of doing something nice, something selfless for Zoe trumped his momentary discomfort. She shouldn't be embarrassed about her financial circumstances. She had a job now. She was responsible. It was time to reconnect with her family.

He pressed the button to buy the voucher.

"Hey, Sean."

He saw a man dressed up as Santa Claus standing next to his table. "Do I know you?"

Behind gold wire-rimmed glasses, the man's blue eyes twinkled. "I know you, Sean Hughes."

Oh, the guy must have recognized him from the news. Sean got a lot of that after high-profile rescues, but news junkies and armchair climbers usually remembered him and liked to talk about certain rescues.

"Mind if I have a seat?" Santa asked.

"Go ahead." Sean guessed Santa must get coffee breaks. "Busy time of the year."

"The busiest, but it'll slow down soon enough." Santa sat and stretched his long booted legs out. "What are you searching for?"

Sean tucked his iPhone in his pocket. "I was just buying a Christmas present for someone I know."

"Someone special?"

"Yeah."

"Remember, only you can give her what she wants. Needs," Santa said mysteriously.

Sean thought about the airline voucher. "I just hope she likes her present."

Santa pushed his glasses back up his nose. "If you give the gift with your heart, she will."

"Is that a line from a greeting card or a fortune cookie?"

"You always say whatever's on your mind." Santa laughed, a boisterous, rich sound that stirred childhood memories of visiting Santa Claus at this same mall.

Sean looked closer at the guy. He looked a little familiar.

Nah. He shook his head. That had been more than twenty years ago. It was just the red suit and white beard.

Santa grinned, his cheeks a rosy pink. "I've always liked that about you."

Sean had the reputation for speaking his mind. That was why the press sought him out for interviews and sound bites. "Thanks."

"Before I go, I want to tell you something." Santa leaned over the table. "Life gives you presents you didn't plan for. All you can do is accept them. Zoe is a gift, Sean. Take good care of her."

"How do you know her—" before he could finish his question, Santa was gone "—name?"

Sean looked around. The sign in front of the North Pole Village where children had their picture taken with Santa said he was feeding the reindeers.

Odd, Sean thought.

"More presents to check off the list." Zoe appeared and set two more shopping bags under the table with the others. She studied him. "You okay?"

He nodded, even though he felt a little off after the visit with Santa.

She glanced at the list. "I'm almost finished. Two more stores, and we can head home."

With that, she bounced away, a spring to her step and a smile on her face.

Home.

Sean realized how much he wanted Zoe home with him. Not just for Christmas, but New Year's and Valentine's and…

On Christmas Eve, Zoe was surrounded. By the sound of the church choir singing, by a sense of hope, peace, and love…and by Sean's entire family, who took up three whole pews at the lovely rustic church. Young cousins and elderly uncles, Aunt Vera in a feathered hat, mothers holding babies and fathers wrangling excited little ones.

Zoe sighed with contentment. Sean sat beside her, his crutches laid flat beneath the rough-hewn log pew in front of them and his arm around her. It felt good, warm and right. Connie was on the other side, her hand clasped with Hank's resting on his thigh.

Zoe loved her family. Being exiled from them had shaken her world. But at this moment, in this church, she was thankful her mother had banished Zoe from home and threatened her trust fund. Otherwise, she wouldn't be here tonight.

With Sean.

Where she belonged.

It wasn't even December twenty-fifth yet, but this had already been the best Christmas ever.

The organ rolled out the opening chords of "Away in a Manger." Anticipation rustled through the pews. Zoe looked inquiringly at Sean. With a smile, he nodded toward the back of the small church.

Zoe caught her breath in delight as children dressed as characters from the Christmas story filed down the aisle. First came the animals—curly haired sheep, cows with little faces peeping out, two older boys stuck together as a camel. Sean chuckled at a shepherd, dragging his tiny toy sheep behind him like a dog on a leash. Wise men in paper crowns and turbans and bathrobes followed. Next, a choir of angels in white dresses with gold wings on their backs and garland halos on their heads floated down the aisle. One angel was sweet little Rebecca, who had made Zoe the star at the tree-trimming party.

All the white reminded Zoe of a wedding, of the floating fabric from a bride's gown. She imagined herself walking down the aisle dressed in white with a lace veil flowing behind her.

A lump the size of Rebecca's halo formed in Zoe's throat.

What was going on? She had never once pictured herself as a bride. Not when she'd been a bridesmaid. Not when the tabloids had claimed she was engaged to someone she'd never even met.

But here... Now...

Her heart stuttered.

Zoe could picture it so clearly. And she knew why. She turned her head to gaze up at Sean.

She wasn't falling in love with him.

She'd fallen.

I love him.

She inhaled deeply and exhaled slowly.

Zoe had come to Oregon running from her past, escaping scandal, stinging from her family's rejection. Determined to prove her mother wrong and regain access to her trust fund, the last thing on Zoe's mind had been romance, let alone finding love and commitment.

But in some ways, her mother had been right.

Zoe had needed to learn to be responsible. In taking care of Sean, she'd learned to take care of herself. In helping him until he could walk, she had learned to stand on her own two feet.

She admired his commitment to his work and family, his connections to the community, the volunteering of his skill and time with OMSAR, his hard work and careful preparation as well as his sense of fun and adventure. Even when he was injured and in pain, he managed to be generous, caring, strong.

She loved that about him.

She loved him.

And he wanted her.

Her heart sighed.

She was glad they'd taken their relationship slowly, getting to know each other. She could be sure this wasn't just another infatuation or mistake. But in striving to be responsible, had she let caution overwhelm her instincts too much?

As the donkey, Mary and Joseph walked down the aisle, Sean looked down at her and smiled, and she knew.

"If a pregnant woman carrying the son of God can't find a room at the inn, there's no hope for the rest of us," he whispered.

Zoe giggled softly.

Contentment welled inside her. Sean accepted her for who she was. She didn't need to change. She could still follow her heart. Only now she would be smarter about it.

She was done pretending, through with playing roles or games. Her pulse raced. She didn't want to keep putting it off. She wanted to tell Sean the truth.

Trepidation grabbed hold of her.

Maybe not the whole truth all at once. He would be shocked and probably hurt. Her real identity would raise certain issues and questions. She had no idea how he would react, but she didn't want protracted explanations about scandals, campaigns and trust funds to overshadow the magic of this special Christmas.

But she would share the most important fact, the most important gift, of all.

Her love.

She loved Sean.

And it was time to tell him so.

Tonight…

No, she'd wait until tomorrow. Christmas day.

Christmas morning dawned with a shower of snowflakes. Sean smiled. A white Christmas for Zoe.

As Denali bounded through the snow outside, he added a

log to the fire. He thought about the long kisses he'd shared with Zoe last night in front of this very fireplace.

Real kisses without an audience.

It had been more than he'd expected. Sean could have pushed for more. Zoe had seemed willing, but he had remembered what she'd said about working for him and being paid a salary. That had made him pull back. He wanted everything with Zoe to be special, to be perfect.

This was new territory for him, and like the times he wanted to climb a new peak, he needed to be ready. Oh, he might not need a topo map, climber beta, weather reports and avalanche forecast, but as with climbing, he wanted to limit exposure, minimize risk and stack the odds in favor of a successful summit attempt.

As much as Sean wanted Zoe, he had to be prepared.

Denali stood at the door. Zoe waded through the wrapping paper from their stocking stuffers strewn about the floor. "I'll let her in."

As Zoe wiped the dog's paws, the fire roared back to life. Colorful flames crackled in his fireplace, vying for attention with the yule log and carols playing on the television screen. Sean sat on the couch with her present on his lap.

"This one's for you," he said.

Her smile lit up her face like the white lights on their Christmas tree. She sat next to him and took the box. "Is it fragile?"

"No."

She shook it. "I don't hear anything."

"Open it."

"If you insist." She ripped off the bow and tore through the wrapping paper.

Sean couldn't remember a better Christmas, not since he'd gotten his first snowboard a couple decades ago. Back then he hadn't realized what an impact that gift would have on his life. Maybe today would be the same with Zoe.

Denali lay on her big floor pillow, chewing on the bone she'd found in her own stocking. Empty plates from their breakfast, cooked by him so the fire department could take it easy this morning, sat on the coffee table.

Zoe stared inside the gift box. "An airline voucher? Not to take this the wrong way, but do you want me to go away?"

The confusion in her eyes belied her attempt at humor.

"I want you to go home and visit your family. Emphasis on visit," he said. "I gave you a voucher because I have no idea where they live so couldn't buy you a roundtrip ticket. I also wanted you to be the one to decide the right time to go."

As she read the voucher, tears spiked her eyelashes. "This…" Her voice cracked. "You didn't have to do this."

I wanted to," he said. "Now there's nothing to stop you from going home."

"Thank you." She cuddled against him, one hand on his chest, and looked up at him. "Maybe you could come with me?"

"I'd like that."

The lyrics of the Christmas carol mentioned home and family. That sounded good to Sean. He held her in his arms. Man, he could get used to this.

"Have you called your mother yet?" he asked.

"No." She snuggled closer. "But I will."

His pulse kicked up a notch as she pressed against him. "Don't forget, it'll be crazy at my parents'. It takes hours to open all the gifts."

Zoe sat up. "I'll call home before we leave."

"I'm interfering."

"Yes, but I understand." She squeezed his hand, sending a tingle up his arm. "It runs in your family."

He laughed.

She glanced at the clock. "Your present will be here in a minute. It's not something I could wrap, but I hope you like it."

He rubbed her back. "Having you here is the best Christmas present."

"I can say the same about you. Though the airline voucher is a very thoughtful gift."

Denali raised her head. She dropped the bone.

"Is someone here, girl?" Sean asked.

The dog trotted to the door.

"Come on." Zoe jumped off the couch. "It's your Christmas present."

As he followed her to the front door, he heard bells jingling. Must be on the television.

As she rested her hand on the door handle, her eyes brimmed with excitement.

"Close your eyes."

Sean did. He felt a rush of cold air, as if someone had opened the door.

"You can open them," she said.

He stared out the front door at a horse-drawn sleigh in his driveway. A large black horse pulled a red-and-green sleigh decorated with a garland. Two old-fashioned lanterns hung off the front. A driver with a stovetop hat and forest-green frock coat held the reins with gloved hands. Denali had already jumped into the sled, ready to go for a ride.

Zoe touched her lips gently to his. "Merry Christmas, Sean."

"Wow. I never would have expected this."

She pulled back to gaze into his eyes, hers wide with hope. "You like it?"

"I love it."

I love you, he thought. But he wasn't ready to say the words just yet. He framed her face with his hands. "This must have been really expensive."

"You're worth it."

"Thank you," he said, choked up. "Thank you so much."

Denali barked from the sled.

Bubbling with excitement, Zoe pulled a bundle of his clothes out of the coat closet. "Put these on."

Insulated pants, down jacket, thermal socks for his feet. "Where are we going?"

She grinned. "It's a surprise."

Soon, they were on their way. Even Denali looked thrilled.

The sleigh took them on a tour around town. Sean cuddled with Zoe under thick wool blankets. He brushed his lips across her forehead. "This is a fantastic way to spend Christmas. A sleigh ride through our own winter wonderland."

"Just wait. The best is yet to come."

Sean didn't doubt it. His parents and family thought she was the perfect match. He had to agree with them. He'd never felt so close to another woman. He'd never wanted to settle down until Zoe. She'd come into his life exactly when he needed her.

He could imagine what would come next—a life together, more stockings hanging on the fireplace. He was ready for the future, a future with her.

CHAPTER TEN

TWENTY minutes later, the sleigh pulled up to a trailhead where a group of snowshoers stood around a bonfire. Sean took a closer look. Not any snowshoers—Jake, Carly, Kendall, Austin, Leanne, Bill and Tim with his young son, Wyatt, in a baby carrier. Just like last year. From their flushed faces, Sean could tell they were just back from their walk.

Maybe we can figure out something.

He'd completely forgotten what Zoe had said that night when the Christmas tree arrived, but she hadn't. Her gesture underscored what he loved about her—her warm, generous heart, her impulsive nature, her understanding of how to have fun. He could only imagine how much she must have spent. She'd probably blown an entire paycheck on this.

On him.

You're worth it.

A lump formed in his throat. Sean couldn't speak.

Zoe held his gloved hand in hers and squeezed. "I know you would have rather gone snowshoeing with everyone, but I hope you don't mind hanging out and having hot cocoa and cookies."

Sean cleared his throat. He felt an odd tingling in the pit of his stomach. "I don't mind."

She smiled.

A good thing he was sitting down, she would have knocked him down with that grin of hers.

He remembered what that Santa guy had said at the mall.

Zoe is a gift, Sean. Take good care of her.

She was a gift, one Sean wanted to cherish and keep.

A ball of warmth settled at the center of his chest. He squeezed her hand. "This is such a special Christmas present."

A satisfied smile lit her face. "Jake helped me with some of the arrangements."

"But it was your idea."

She nodded, a little shy.

"Thank you." He kissed her. "I can't wait to see how you top this gift next year."

Her eyes widened again. Her breath caught. "Next year?"

Did she understand, Sean wondered, that he wasn't joking, wasn't pretending, wasn't playing games any longer?

She smiled. "I'm sure I'll come up with something."

Sean thought about not only spending next Christmas with Zoe, but also the 365 days in between.

"But I still have something else for you this year," she said.

"You've given me so much already."

"I want to give you this." Zoe took a deep breath and another. She gazed deeply into his eyes. "Sean, I love you."

His heart jolted. The air rushed from his lungs. A fire lit in his gut.

Best Christmas, ever. Hands down.

He touched her cheek. "I love you, too."

She grinned, the blue of her eyes sparkling. "Just remember who went all in first."

Zoe had told Sean she would call her mother. She knew she needed to, but still she hesitated. A part of her worried what her mother would say.

Christmas had been perfect so far. Sean loved her. She didn't want to ruin everything by having to hear her mother's disapproving voice.

But it was Christmas. Zoe had to call. She picked up the telephone only to set it down again.

Pathetic.

If Sean and the rest of the Hughes had taught her anything this past month, it was the importance of family. She needed to do this.

No more pretenses. No more being who she wasn't.

Despite their differences, she loved her mother. And that meant sharing a few basic, important things with the governor. Like phone calls on Christmas.

Or the fact that Zoe had fallen in love.

She called her mother's personal number. The phone rang and rang.

Relief mingled with disappointment. She continued to let it ring so it would switch her over to voice mail. At least she could leave a message.

"Vanessa Carrington," a stately female voice said.

Anxiety shot through Zoe. "Merry Christmas, Mother."

"Zoe. How good to hear from you," she said. "We got your presents. It was very thoughtful of you. You'll see some extra money deposited in your account. We all thought that would be more practical than gifts."

Zoe smiled wryly to herself. She thought about the number of presents under Connie and Hank's tree with her name on them. But Zoe knew her family meant well. "Thanks."

"How are you doing?" Vanessa asked with genuine concern.

"Fine." Zoe hesitated. "But Mother…I've met someone."

"A man?"

"Yes." She held her breath.

"Zoe."

The disapproval in that one word made her cringe. "It's not like that, Mother. I know I'd say that anyway, but he's different from the others. His name is Sean Hughes. He owns a snowboarding company in Oregon. I met him on Thanksgiving Day. He broke his leg. I've been taking care of him."

"Well, I… Are you living with him? In his house?"

"Yes, but it's not what you're thinking," Zoe explained. "I'm working for him. With a salary. Under the circumstances, we haven't... We've kept that part of our relationship professional."

"I don't know what to say."

"Maybe...that you're happy for me?"

"I am, of course, but Zoe...do you need money?"

A familiar frustration gnawed at her. The old Zoe would have cringed or slammed the phone down. Not the new Zoe. "No, Mother, that's not why I called. I'm fine. I've earned enough that I haven't had to touch my allowance this month."

"That's very responsible of you."

"I'm learning," she admitted. "It isn't easy taking care of somebody. Or myself. Maybe now I have a better understanding of what you must have gone through with me. Especially after Dad died."

"My goodness. You sound different," Vanessa said. "More mature. If this is the influence of your...new man, I approve."

"Thanks."

"I mean it." Her mother's voice warmed. "Merry Christmas. Perhaps, since you've learned your lesson, it's time you come home."

"I'm staying in Oregon."

"Why would you want to do that?"

Zoe thought about the smile on Sean's face when he realized the second part of his present. Or the way he kissed her while they sat at the bonfire with his friends. Her friends now. Or the way he planned on her being with him next Christmas. Joy overflowed from her heart. "I'm in love with Sean."

The line went silent.

Zoe gripped the receiver. "Mother?"

"Love?" her mother's voice rose two octaves. "You can't be in love. When did you say you met him? Thanksgiving?"

"I'll admit it hasn't been that long, but I know what I'm

doing," Zoe said firmly. "There's nothing that will make me change my mind."

"Nothing?"

"Nothing. Not even my trust fund," she reiterated to drive home the point.

"Because of this man? What's his name?"

"Sean Hughes. Yes, it's because of him, but it's also because of me. I finally know who I am. What I want."

"He could be after your money. I'd hate for you to have your heart broken again. I'll have him investigated."

"There's no need, Mom," Zoe explained. "Sean has a successful company. His family has lived in the area forever. They're very well-known, liked, down-to-earth. No skeletons in the closet."

Only a lot of ex-girlfriends.

But she had her share of ex-boyfriends.

"This sounds serious." Her mother sounded more concerned than ever. "Why don't you bring him home so your brothers and I can meet him?"

"He's still recovering from his fall, Mom," Zoe said. "He has a tib-fib fracture. It's healing, but traveling might be too hard on him."

"You are more responsible."

"I'm trying to be, but I'm still me, too."

"Well, you," Vanessa said. "It sounds like I need to come to you, then. How does the twenty-eighth sound?"

Zoe gulped. "That's only three days away. Why don't you wait until after the holidays?"

"I don't want to wait. E-mail my assistant your contact info," Vanessa said. "I'll let you know when all the arrangements have been confirmed."

"Sure."

"Dinner's ready so I have to go," Vanessa said. "Have a Merry Christmas, Zoe. I love you."

"I love you, too, Mother."

Zoe hung up the phone.

Her mother, the venerable Vanessa Carrington, would be here in three days.

What in the world was Zoe going to tell Sean?

Talk about a magical Christmas.

Sitting in his parents' living room, Sean smiled at the scene around him. Flames crackled in the fireplace. The scent of ham lingered in the air. Colorful ribbons and bows lay strewn on the carpet. Kids ran around with their new toys and smiles as bright as the lights on the nine-foot-tall Nobel fir tree. But his favorite part was Zoe.

She'd seemed nervous, a little distracted, after her phone call with her mother, but all of that seemed to disappear once they'd arrived here and his family pulled her into their holiday craziness.

He put his arm around Zoe. "Enjoying yourself?"

Her blue eyes sparkled, matching the new knit scarf she wore around her neck. "This is the best Christmas ever."

"Yes, it is."

Not even his mother's not-so-subtle hints about how special it would be if he proposed right there at the Christmas celebration bothered him. Truth was, a marriage proposal didn't seem like such a crazy idea any longer.

She loved him. He loved her.

More mistletoe appeared over them, compliments of Aunt Vera. There was no longer any awkwardness about kissing under it, no more pretense or lies. This was for real. He'd never felt so relaxed and happy.

Sean kissed Zoe firmly on the lips, as if they had been together forever, not just since Thanksgiving.

She stared at him with suddenly misty eyes. "I wish today didn't have to end."

"I know, but New Year's is only a week away." Sean had a lot of work to do between now and then. He cuddled with Zoe. "Why don't you come with me to the Rail Jam Extravaganza so we can ring in the New Year together?"

* * *

The next morning, Zoe stood in the bathroom. She stared at her reflection in the mirror.

"Sean," she said aloud. "There's something I need to tell you. Flynn is actually my middle name. My last name is really Carrington. My mother is Governor Vanessa Carrington. You may have heard of her. And me."

Lame. Zoe shook her head.

Thank goodness her mother didn't arrive for two more days. Maybe by then Zoe would know what to say to Sean.

"Zoe." His voice sounded different. Urgent. Anxious.

She hurried down the stairs. "Are you okay?"

Sean nodded once. He stood on his crutches. "The call for a rescue mission just went out. I need to head to the base camp and help."

Just for a moment, she wondered what he thought he could do with two bad legs. But she bit her tongue.

"Sure," Zoe said. "Let's go."

"I can hop a ride with Jake."

"No. I want to be there. With you," she said, so there could be no misunderstanding. "This is an important part of your life. I want to know what you do up there."

A muscle flicked at his jaw. "I won't be up there."

Hearing his frustration, she touched his arm. She knew how important his rescue work was to him, how responsible he felt for the men and women he worked with. "Not today, but with the progress you're already making, you'll be up there soon enough. It'll be better if I have an idea of what's going on before that happens."

Some of the tension left his face. He tugged on her braid. "Come on."

"Do I need to bring anything?"

"Patience," he said. "Maybe some prayers. A book wouldn't be a bad idea, either. It could be a long day."

She stared up at him, her heart full of love. "As long as I'm with you, it won't matter."

He shrugged on his OMSAR jacket. "Oh, didn't you want to talk to me about something?"

"Yes," she admitted. "But it can wait."

"There's another weather system moving in." Sean, acting as the PIO, public information officer, spoke to the media at the base of rescue operations. He would rather have been on the mountain. But he was happy to contribute in any way he could, and he was comfortable in the public eye. Good thing, too, as the number of microphones and cameras kept increasing as more information about the missing climbers was released. "According to NOAA, the winds will increase to eighty-five miles per hour. The rescue teams on the mountain have a turnaround time of two o'clock to make sure they're out of danger."

"What about the missing climbers?" a local news station reporter asked. "Won't those winds be dangerous for them?"

"Rescuer safety is our first priority," Sean explained. "We are attempting to regain contact with the missing climbers."

He glanced at the back of the room for Zoe, but she had slipped away. He didn't blame her. The media storm was pretty intimidating for anyone who wasn't used to it.

"So to confirm what we know," a radio reporter said. "A father and his two teenage sons, ages seventeen and fourteen, are missing somewhere on Mount Hood."

"Correct," Sean said.

"Do you know if both boys are injured?" a journalist for the Portland daily paper inquired.

"We are still trying to confirm the extent of the injuries for each of the subjects." Sean noticed the IC, incident commander, gesturing to him. "The teams will continue their search until the turnaround time. We'll have another briefing at fourteen hundred. Thank you."

He hurried over to the IC and waited while the man ended a cell phone call. "Any word?" Sean asked.

"No, all the snowfall overnight is making it hard to see anything," the IC said. "This is going national. CNN, FOX, MSNBC."

That meant phone interviews until they got their crews out here or piggybacked with one of the local news affiliates.

"It's going to turn into a real circus," the IC added.

"No worries," Sean reassured him. "It's nothing we haven't dealt with before. Or won't deal with again."

The lines of IC's face relaxed. "Nice to have you down here for once, Hughes. Though I know you'd rather be up there."

Sean thought about the teams up there. Yeah, that was where he wanted to be, too, but until he was a hundred percent recovered, he would only be a liability. At least his effort down here freed an able-bodied person to do the real rescue work. "Happy to help out where I can."

"I need to go and check with the safety officer."

"I'll prepare for the interviews." Sean sat at a table with notes about the mission objectives, the number of teams in the field and the three subjects. A steaming cup of black coffee appeared in front of him. "Just what I needed."

Zoe placed her hands on his shoulders. "Caffeine works wonders."

He leaned back against her and felt the beating of her heart. "I wasn't talking about the coffee."

She kissed the top of his head. "Just tell me what you need."

"That's easy." Sean wished he could send some of the warmth he felt right now to the teams in the field. Up on the mountain, the risk of frostbite was high. "All I need is you."

All he would ever need.

Sean wasn't about to let Zoe get away from him. He would have to see about getting his grandmother's ring out of the bank safe-deposit box. Just to be prepared...

A traditional girl like Zoe deserved a traditional proposal. That would take planning and preparation. Right now, he needed to focus on the missing climbers and rescue mission.

She massaged his shoulders. "Things are tense around here."

"With the weather changing again, the teams will have to come down."

"I can't imagine what that father and his two sons must be going through up there. Injured. Stuck on the mountain." She shivered. "I can't shake the sound of that teenager's voice during the 911 call."

"The kid's keeping it together given what happened," Sean said, impressed with what he'd heard in a call from the fourteen-year-old. "Now that we've lost contact... You know, I was the same age the first time my dad took me up Hood. I remember what he told me as we were preparing for the climb. He said, 'Son, there are old climbers and there are bold climbers, but there are no old bold climbers.' Climbing with your dad is great, and it should never turn out like this."

"They'll find them." Zoe pressed against him. "It's only the twenty-sixth of December. There has to be some Christmas magic left on the mountain."

Sean turned and kissed her quickly on the lips. "Maybe we can send some of our magic up to them."

"Your kisses are pretty magical." She smiled. "So is the way you handle the press. They adore you. I have a feeling a photograph of you hugging the boys' mom will be on the front page of the paper tomorrow."

"I didn't know you were watching me." He took a sip of his coffee. "Every time the press appears, you disappear."

"Just trying to stay out of the way."

"Well, I'm really glad you're here."

"Me, too." Zoe smiled at him. "I'm getting an idea of what you do, and the precautions you take to make sure everyone stays safe. I'm impressed."

Her willingness to lend a hand, do whatever needed to be done, warmed and impressed him. "You'll make a fine associate member."

"That's what Will said." He had been working here at the

base, too. Not for OMSAR, but the sheriff's office. "He also said cooking wasn't a membership requirement."

Sean laughed. "A good thing in your case."

"Hey, I can learn," Zoe said. "Remember, I got five cookbooks from your family for Christmas."

"And two fire extinguishers."

She grinned. "Well, you like to be prepared, and your family is getting to know me well."

A loud commotion sounded. Streaks of light flashed. The noise level rose exponentially.

Zoe looked at him, her nose crinkled. "I didn't think you had another press conference scheduled until later."

"We don't." Sean rose. He would have heard if the status had changed. "I better find out what's going on. Come on."

"I don't mind staying here."

"Humor me."

Zoe pulled her ski cap so low he could barely see her face. "Okay."

"There's no reason for you to hide." He tugged on her hat. "Unless you're wearing something that says OMSAR, even someone as pretty as you is safe from the media frenzy."

He entered the cafeteria to see Will, in full deputy's uniform, escorting a stylish older woman.

Will motioned to him. "This is Sean Hughes, Governor."

Governor? Not of Oregon, that was for sure. But the woman's face looked a little familiar. Still, Sean couldn't place her.

"It's so nice to meet you, Sean." The woman's wide smile reached her blue eyes. "Zoe's told me a little about you."

"Zoe…"

"Mother?" Zoe sounded horrified. "What are you doing here?"

Mother? Sean's gaze darted between the two. He could kind of see a resemblance. Straight nose. Full mouth. Maybe that accounted for the familiarity of her face? But Zoe and her family were estranged.

"Visiting, dear," the woman said.

"You said you wouldn't be here for two more days."

"I know, but I wanted to see you so I decided to come today."

"You left Maxwell's house early to come see me?"

The surprise in Zoe's voice, the hope in her eyes, nearly broke Sean's heart, even though he was really confused and still reeling from their introduction. What did Will mean calling her Governor? Governor Flynn?

The woman nodded. "I wanted to see you and meet Sean."

Zoe ran to her mother's open arms.

A flash captured the moment.

Zoe drew back as if she'd been covered in acid, not light.

"Don't worry, dear," her mother said gently. "It's okay."

Not wanting to interrupt, but needing to know what was going on, Sean cleared his throat.

"I'm Vanessa Carrington." The older woman extended her arm. Her nails were polished. Her skin soft. "It's so nice to meet you, Sean."

Not Flynn. Carrington. He knew who Governor Carrington was. Most people did. The then-wife-now-widow of a multimillionaire who'd decided to give politics a whirl. The mother of a flighty socialite. He'd seen the stories on *E!* and in the tabloids at the supermarket. Sexy blond party girl Zoe...

Carrington.

He stared at Zoe, hoping for some other explanation.

She hunched her shoulders. "Flynn is my middle name. I'm really Zoe Carrington."

The missing socialite. The wild child. The other woman.

But that couldn't be the same sweet brunette who burned food, danced in the snow, walked his dog and played with his cousins' kids.

No way. Not his Zoe. Someone had to be pulling a prank.

He looked again from the governor's well-preserved jawline and expertly made-up face to Zoe's. He could still see that resemblance between the governor and her. Around the nose and mouth.

Sean glanced at Will, who looked as surprised as he was.

"I was planning to tell you, but…" Zoe glanced at the curious media with a look of fear in her eyes.

Sean might be confused, but Zoe was scared. Trembling. He needed to protect her. "Hey, baby, it's going to be okay."

It had to be okay. This was the woman he wanted to spend the rest of his life with.

"Look, it's Zoe Carrington," someone yelled.

"She's with Sean Hughes," another shouted.

The media rushed forward like a wave about to pound the shore. Will stepped in front of the governor, placing himself between her and the horde of reporters while her security detail scrambled to get closer.

"I'm so sorry, Sean," Zoe mumbled.

"Let's just give them what they want." Governor Carrington smoothed her jacket and adjusted her scarf. "Then they'll leave us alone."

Sean didn't think a sound bite or two would satisfy that hungry crowd.

"Whatever you think best, Mother." Zoe sounded different. Polished. She readjusted her hat, combed through her hair with her fingers and pinched her cheeks to give them color.

He stared in disbelief at the sudden change in her.

"Ready, Sean?" Vanessa asked.

Will gave him a sympathetic look.

Zoe's blue eyes implored him.

Sean would do this for her. "Sure."

Will raised a hand to quiet the mob. "Governor Carrington will take a few questions now."

The press jockeyed for positions. Flashes blinded them. Lights blared down on them. Cameras rolled. A bouquet of microphones was shoved toward their faces.

Sean wasn't a stranger to the press, but all this was rather disconcerting. The governor acted as if this were nothing. Zoe stood as still as a statue.

"Good afternoon," Governor Carrington announced to the media. "Our prayers are with the missing climbers, the rescuers on the mountain and all of their families today."

"You're in the middle of a tough campaign for a coveted U.S. Senate seat," a woman reporter asked. "What brings you to Mount Hood only a few weeks before the special election?"

"My youngest child. My daughter, Zoe, has been staying in Oregon." The governor smiled at her and Sean. "I'm here to support her and someone who is very special to the Carrington family."

Sean stiffened at the implication of her words. Okay, it might be true, but he didn't like the way she'd announced it to the world. His arm slipped from around Zoe's waist.

"How long have you been in Oregon, Zoe?" someone shouted.

"Since mid-November." She flashed a flirty smile. "I've been staying in Hood Hamlet for almost a month now."

A reporter scribbled a note. "Right under our noses."

No, right under his. Sean stared at her.

"Well, I'd hoped it was the one place you wouldn't suspect, and you didn't." Zoe was transforming before his eyes from the sweet woman who took care of him to first daughter without the slightest hesitation. He was stunned by the way she handled the media like a pro, teasing and flirting as if she'd done it her entire life. It was weird and unsettling to see her act this way. "Though I had to hide when some of you interviewed Sean at the hospital."

So that was why she hadn't been in his hospital room, he realized. One question answered, but more kept surfacing.

Where was the woman he'd fallen in love with? Who was the woman standing next to him?

Sean felt totally blindsided. He wanted answers. He wanted them now.

"You could have told us, Sean," a reporter he knew well said.

Survival and self-preservation instincts kicked in. "I wanted to keep Zoe all to myself."

"I don't blame you there."

"He also has been a little preoccupied with his recovery," Zoe added.

"And you?" someone yelled from the back of the crowd.

Zoe smiled coquettishly.

Talk about the press conference from hell. Sean gripped his crutches so tightly his knuckles turned white.

"What are your plans, Governor?" a woman shouted.

"Well, I want to spend a little time with my daughter." Vanessa smiled at Sean. "And I'd also like to see if I can convince Sean to fly back east and join us on the campaign trail for a few days."

Join them where? Sean's temper flared.

"What do you think about that, Sean? You ready to leave the mountain for politics?" a radio reporter asked.

Hell, no, was how Sean wanted to answer, and he would have except he didn't want to hurt Zoe. Instead, he motioned to his crutches. A perfect excuse. "I'm not sure I'd be much help in my current condition."

Zoe stared at him with gratitude in her eyes. "But once Sean's back at one hundred percent, there'll be no stopping him."

"What about Lonzo Green?" another reporter called out.

The married actor? Sean looked at Zoe.

She held her head high. "You should talk to his wife if you want information about him, not me."

A reporter held a digital tape recorder. "How do you feel about Zoe's colorful past, Sean?"

"The only thing that matters is the present," he answered.

"Governor? Any comment?"

Vanessa Carrington beamed. "Of course, I'm delighted

with Zoe's choice. Sean's going to fit into the family just fine."

His jaw worked. So, Zoe had an interfering mother. So did he. Sean could live with that. But at least his family's expectations had always been expressed in private. He'd never expected—he'd sure as hell never wanted—some media-savvy governor presenting him to the press as some kind of "first-son-in-law" and wanting to take him on the campaign trail.

Sean motioned to Will, who stepped in and called a halt to the press conference. "That's all, people."

"What is going on?" Will whispered, as the media dispersed.

"I have no idea," Sean said grimly.

The deputy glanced at Zoe, who was huddled with her mother. "You didn't know?"

"Nope."

"Damn."

That was putting it lightly.

Zoe walked over to him. "Are you ready to go home?"

Sean's pride was hurt and his faith in his judgment was shaken. He felt used by both Zoe and her mother.

"The mission is still going on," he said tightly. "I can't leave."

She stared up at him with wide eyes. "But…we need to talk."

"Not now. I don't have the time."

"But—"

"Three climbers are missing." He couldn't control his temper any longer. "I have a responsibility here. A role. This is what I need to focus on right now. Not this. Not you. Go home."

"I can't leave." She touched his arm. "You need me."

"No." He jerked away. "I don't."

CHAPTER ELEVEN

ZOE DELAYED taking Denali for a walk until the rescue was reported on FOX News. A rescue team had found the missing climbers, a father and two sons. The three missing climbers were suffering from frostbite and broken limbs, but at least they were alive. A happy ending, the anchor concluded joyfully.

A last moment of Christmas magic, Zoe thought.

Standing in the snow with Sean's dog, she blotted her eyes and blew her nose, grateful and miserable at the same time.

Her feelings were hurt, but she knew Sean had a tendency to overdo it; however, with three lives on the line, his preoccupation was justified. Still she needed a sprinkle of that Christmas magic herself right now.

You need me.

No, I don't.

She whistled for Denali and headed back to the house.

I don't need you.

"Sean's back." Vanessa met them in the foyer, her usually severe face sympathetic. "I'm going to be in the study checking my e-mail and making phone calls so the two of you can talk."

"Thanks, Mother."

With a deep breath, Zoe walked into the great room to find Sean sitting on the couch. But the man who'd needed her help getting to the bathroom or washing or dressing was gone, replaced by an almost stranger with a determined set of his jaw and hard lines on his face.

She'd done this to him. To them.

The realization clawed at her heart.

Zoe walked toward him intent on making things better. She sat next to him. "I'm sorry, Sean. I've been meaning to tell you the truth. That's what I wanted to talk to you about."

"You should have told me." Sean shook his head. "I felt ambushed today."

"I know." She stared at the floor. "I wanted to tell you the truth right away, but I was afraid someone might find out who I was or where I was. My mother threatened to cut off access to my trust fund if I didn't straighten up and be more responsible."

"Trust fund? I figured out your family had money, but I didn't think you did. So you needing a job, a place to stay, were more lies."

"No. I wasn't lying about any of that." Zoe lowered her voice. "My mother put me on a limited allowance. I had hardly any money left when I met you. You really helped me out."

"I thought we saw each other for who we are." He stared at the fireplace. "But I haven't a clue who you are."

"I'm still me. Zoe. My last name doesn't change that." She scooted toward him, but he moved away. Her heart felt as if it had cracked. "I figured out who I was being here with you. The real Zoe. One I like and am proud to be."

"The real Zoe?" he repeated. "Everything was based on a lie."

Under the hurt, she felt a flash of temper. "I agreed to be your pretend girlfriend. Continuing the charade for your family was your idea."

"Exactly. My idea. I knew what was going on. We both knew what we were getting into." He grimaced. "You agreed to the lies we told my family, but I never signed on for this."

"I didn't lie to you. I just didn't tell you everything."

"I trusted you. Do you know how it felt not to know who the

woman standing next to me at the press conference was? She looked like you, but she sure as hell didn't act like you."

"My mother has been governor since I was eight," Zoe tried to explain. "Everything from my father's death to my brothers' weddings has been covered by the press. I was taught to act that way when I was a little girl. It's second nature. I can't help it."

He rose. "What else don't I know about you, Zoe?"

"What do you want to know? My secrets? The lies printed about me in the tabloids and gossip blogs?" Tears pricked her eyes. "Who I've been with you is who I am. I just didn't know it until coming here. Listen to your heart. You know me, Sean."

"I'm not so sure anymore."

Her heart split open. "I love you."

The three words spilled from her lips as if they could make this all better, make things go back to the way they were this morning.

He didn't say anything.

"Sean…"

"You're asking me to accept a completely different vision of you with short notice and no preparation." He used his crutches to cross the room, to get away from her. Denali followed him. "You've sprung this on me at the worst possible time. I'm just getting my life back on track. Recovering. Working. I can't be distracted right now. I have the Rail Jam Extravaganza on New Year's. That's a priority for me."

"And I'm not." Zoe fought the urge to say something hurtful and run out of the room. Her insides trembled and tears welled in her eyes, yet she remained in control. She wasn't that same, old Zoe. "I've heard that before."

From her mother, her brothers, boyfriends and friends. Zoe wanted to believe Sean wasn't like the other people in her life. She wanted to be his priority, but maybe that wasn't possible right now. Still, she knew he needed her. Not to take care of him because of his injuries, but to love him. The way she needed him to love her in return.

"You need time," she said.

He nodded.

"Fine." Zoe's heart ached, but she would give Sean what he wanted. "You gave me time when I asked for it. I can give you that now. Time and space so you can focus. I'll go home with my mother."

And wait.

Who the hell was Zoe Carrington?

Three days later, Sean was alone with his thoughts and his dog. He'd sent his family away, rejected his friends' offers to come over with beer and sympathy. Not even work was filling the void. He hadn't realized there'd been a black hole in his life until Zoe left. Sean wanted to be alone to nurse his leg and his grievances.

He stared morosely into the empty fireplace. Was this how the women he'd broken up with felt? He'd been a player. Zoe had played him good.

He grabbed his laptop, went to Google and searched for her name. Over sixteen million results appeared, everything from evocative images to a wikipedia entry.

Some of the entries made him sick. The coverage of her and the married actor that seemed to catapult the guy's career to A-list. An NFL quarterback who claimed she'd stalked him only to whine when he heard she was dating someone else. Car accidents and run-ins with the paparazzi that resulted in confidential, out-of-court settlements.

No doubt there were two sides to each story. He couldn't bring himself to believe the woman he'd been living with for the past month was capable of the motives attributed to her by the media.

Sean remembered Zoe saying she'd been dealing with this since she was eight. No wonder she'd developed ways to cope.

He selected News.

One headline read Governor Carrington to Host Final New Year's Eve Ball.

He scanned the article about the term-limited governor's last big hurrah, her final New Year's party to be held in the governor's mansion. The story mentioned Zoe was expected to attend the highly anticipated soiree.

Other stories mentioned only Zoe's name, nothing about what she'd been doing or where she'd been. Even the gossip bloggers posted that Zoe continued to keep a low presence since returning home from her "travels."

Strange. If Zoe was such a wild child, why hadn't she returned to the same party scene she'd left in Los Angeles? Why wasn't she hanging out with her old friends making up for lost time?

Sean focused on one image that had caught his eye. A picture of a blonde climbing out of a cab in front of a club back in September, but superimposed on her face were the eyes, the smile of the woman he loved. He tried to reconcile the party girl in the skimpy green dress with the woman he knew.

Zoe Carrington. Zoe Flynn.

Blonde. Brunette.

Homewrecker. Homebody.

The two women were supposedly one and the same. Yet...

Who I've been with you is who I am. I just didn't know it until coming here. Listen to your heart. You know me, Sean.

Zoe's words swirled through his brain. He stared again at the photo, into her eyes, remembering what the Santa guy had said at the mall.

Life gives you presents you didn't plan for. All you can do is accept them. Zoe is a gift, Sean. Take good care of her.

She had accepted him, but he hadn't done the same with her. That was when he realized...

Her last name didn't matter. Her last name didn't change anything.

He did know her.

Sean looked around the room and saw the big, tall

Christmas tree with all the homemade ornaments she'd helped the kids make. His gaze focused on one in particular, a star that Rebecca had made.

He knew Zoe's compassion, her creativity and her ability to stand up to him when needed. He also knew her heart, her giving, nurturing thoughtful heart.

She'd accepted his past while he...

What had he done?

Zoe, no matter her last name, was everything he needed. All he needed. The woman he loved.

But his pride hadn't let him see it.

For weeks the two of them had talked about everything, but when finally faced with the fact Zoe had a life outside of their little world, Sean had shut down. He hadn't wanted to listen to her.

He'd been upset. Hurt. Stupid.

He had to go after her. Apologize. Make her see that she didn't have to be Zoe Carrington or Zoe Flynn. She could just be Zoe. His Zoe. Zoe Hughes.

But how?

Sean dragged his hand over his face.

He thought about what Zoe might have done in this situation. She would have followed her instincts, acted impulsively, made a grand gesture.

Like the sleigh ride on Christmas day.

He needed to take a page from her playbook and do the same thing, to go all in even if he wasn't holding the right cards and sure he would win.

Sean thought for a moment. He remembered reading about a New Year's ball. That would be a grand gesture, but he had the Rail Jam Extravaganza to attend at the same time. He was the face of Hughes Snowboards. He'd built his business by making that kind of public appearance a priority.

And I'm not. I've heard that before.

He stared at Zoe's image.

She'd said enough about her past for him to realize her

family had never made time for her. He didn't want to be like them. He couldn't be like them.

Zoe deserved better.

He'd never made time for a woman before, but Sean wanted to convince Zoe that she was a priority in his life. No matter what it took.

Sean rose, tried to take a step and fell back onto the couch.

In his hurry to make things right, he'd forgotten about his crutches, about his leg.

He couldn't do this on his own. He was going to need help to pull this off. Sean picked up the phone and started punching in numbers.

On New Year's Eve, Zoe eyed the enormous clock set above the stage in the ballroom, counting down the hours and minutes until midnight. The band tuned up. Ice sculptures dripped and gleamed. Fragrant and colorful flower arrangements decorated the linen-covered tables. Everything was in place for a spectacular start to a Happy New Year.

But Sean wasn't here.

He hadn't contacted her in the five days since she'd left Hood Hamlet. Not a word, a voice message, an e-mail, a postcard.

Zoe worried how he was doing, whether he was taking care of himself or overdoing it, and if he'd hired someone else to help him out. She hadn't really expected to hear from him with the Rail Jam Extravaganza coming up, but still, she'd hoped.

She was being mature, but she wanted to pout like a child. She wanted to be a part of his life, but he'd made it clear she wasn't an important part.

A lump formed in her throat.

She had agreed to give him time. Maybe now that she'd left Hood Hamlet, Sean had decided he didn't have time for a relationship. He wanted his life to be like it was before his fall.

Her heart squeezed.

"Can you believe it's New Year's Eve?" Vanessa Carrington sashayed toward her across the shining ballroom floor in the governor's mansion. "I know this has been a difficult week for you, Zoe. But I'm happy you're home and here tonight."

"Thanks, Mother." Zoe forced a smile and pressed her cheek to her mother's powdered and perfumed one. "The room looks wonderful."

"Thanks to you. I'm so pleased you spoke with the event planner. You really have a good eye." The echo of Sean's words touched Zoe's heart. "And speaking of lovely..." Vanessa motioned for her to spin around. "That blue is very flattering."

"Thanks."

The look in her mother's eyes softened. "I know you miss him, but it's New Year's Eve. I hope you'll try to have fun tonight."

Zoe had to laugh. "I can't believe you're telling me to have fun."

"Well, I am." Vanessa placed her hands on her hips. "Don't think about Sean. We can deal with that later. You've worked so hard on this party. It's time you enjoyed yourself."

Zoe had thrown herself into the party because she didn't want to think about all she'd left behind in Hood Hamlet. She missed the small town, the people, even the mountain.

Mostly, though, she missed Sean.

Still she couldn't put her life on hold indefinitely. Once, maybe, but not now. She had plans to make. He had taught her the value of that. As soon as the holidays were over, she was putting her résumé and a portfolio together. She'd be prepared whether she heard from Sean or not.

Maxwell, her oldest brother, appeared. He wore a black tuxedo. With his hair slicked back, he looked like the scion of politicians that he was. "The guests are starting to arrive, Mother."

"Thank you, dear." Vanessa extended her hand to Zoe. "Shall we?"

Zoe straightened, smiled and took hold of her mother's hand. "Let's party."

The limousine drove through a neighborhood of large, old houses covered with colorful lights and inflatable decorations in the front yards. The homes might have been bigger, but they made Sean think of Peacock Lane, a Portland neighborhood that took decorating for the holidays to the extreme.

"I don't know about you guys." Bill sprawled out on the backseat of the limo. "I might look like a million dollars, but I feel like a penguin in this monkey suit."

Tim adjusted his bowtie. "Well, you look like a monkey."

The limousine turned left and drove through a gated entrance. Sean stopped toying with the cuff links on his white, starched shirt and stared. A mansion, set back, was lit by thousands of white, twinkling lights.

His heart pounded in his chest.

"Get a load of that." Jake whistled. "We're a long way from Hood Hamlet, boys."

No kidding. Sean stared at the house—it didn't seem a big enough word—where Zoe had grown up. At one point, he'd thought she was homeless. He would have never imagined she'd spent the past sixteen years of her life living in a modern day palace.

"Too bad Will isn't here in case we get into trouble," Tim said.

Bill nodded. "No 'get out of jail free' card for crashing the governor's ball."

"We aren't crashing," Sean said.

Three pairs of eyes turned to him.

"I called in a few favors, gave away a couple boards," Sean explained to their surprised faces. "It wasn't going to do us any good to show up at the door and not be let in. We're on the guest list."

"Always prepared," Jake said.

"Team leader extraordinaire," Tim agreed.

"Cool, now we can eat and drink and not feel guilty," Bill quipped. "Joking."

"You ready, Sean?" Jake asked.

He nodded, still staring at the house. Zoe was inside, somewhere. His objective—to find her. "That's a lot of area to search."

"Don't worry," Tim said. "This is nothing compared to a few of the places we've had to look."

"True that," Jake agreed.

"I still can't believe your wives let you come." Bill fiddled with buttons. The television turned on. The lights dimmed. "On New Year's Eve, no less."

"Carly told me she'd never forgive me if I didn't help," Jake said.

Tim nodded. "Mine said the same thing and added I'd better not screw this up for Sean."

The limousine stopped next to the front steps. A uniformed attendant opened the door.

"Let's do this," Sean said, as if they were about to head into a whiteout rather than a black-tie, by-invitation-only event.

The four of them exited the limousine, feeling like fish out of water. Their normal tools and uniforms were on the other side of the country. No backpacks, helmets, ropes, ice axes and well-worn boots. They had to make do with tuxedos, cuff links, bowties, cummerbunds and shiny, tight shoes.

"No matter what happens." Sean adjusted the crutches under his arms. "Thanks for backing me up on this, dudes."

Jake patted him on the shoulder. "Our pleasure."

Bill rang the doorbell. "Gentlemen, it's showtime."

Inside, women in fancy, long dresses and guys in tuxedos mingled. A real live band—with brass and plenty of soul—played from an elevated stage at one end of the room. Guests sat at linen-covered tables, eating, or stood and drank.

"I don't see her." Sean scanned the crowd. He had no idea if Zoe would still be a brunette or have gone back to blond or some other color. "Let's split up. We can search a larger perimeter that way. Rendezvous back in fifteen minutes."

Fifteen minutes later, no one had seen her.

Jake met his eyes. Shrugged. "No luck."

Sean needed luck. His chest tightened. He needed... Christmas magic.

"It's a big place," Tim consoled him. "Let's expand the search area."

"Zoe would be at the party if she were here." He looked around once more. Still nothing. "Grab a drink and some food. I'm going to make one more pass before calling it."

The others headed to the bar.

Sean rounded a corner and bumped into Governor Carrington.

Her eyes widened when she saw him. "Sean?"

"Hello, Governor."

"Vanessa."

"Vanessa," he corrected.

"Well, look at you." Her once-over made him feel as if he were on display at a fashion show or something. "Not quite the mountain man today."

Sean shrugged. "When in Rome..."

"You fit into Rome quite nicely."

"Uh, thanks. I came to talk to Zoe, but I can't find her."

Vanessa glanced around. "She's here somewhere."

Sean straightened, every nerve ending stood at attention. "Zoe may not want to talk to me."

"Oh, she'll talk to you." The governor motioned to two large doors. "Zoe might be out there. She used to hide on the balcony during parties when she was a little girl." A soft smile formed on Vanessa's face. "She's still my little girl, Sean. But I hope everything works out the way you want it to."

"Even if it means I take Zoe back with me to Oregon?" he asked.

Vanessa nodded. "Even then."

"Thanks."

Sean glanced at the big clock over the stage. Almost time.

With a deep breath, he propped open the balcony door and swung outside on his crutches.

Standing on the balcony on the chilly, overcast night, Zoe ignored the goose bumps on her arms and how cold her toes were. Instead, she stared at the lights twinkling in the nearby neighborhood. They reminded her of stars.

Stars.

Her breath caught in her throat.

I grew up with multicolored lights, but the white ones look like stars to me.

Sean.

Her chest constricted.

She remembered the glittery star ornament little Rebecca had made for her. Zoe had left it on the tree, thinking she would be back.

If only she could wish upon a star now for what her heart desired....

But Christmas was over. All the magic had been used up. No more miracles to be had.

She clutched the railing, disappointed and hurting.

That time on the mountain was over. She was back in the governor's mansion, back in the public eye. She was happy to be reconciled with her mother and brothers, but she couldn't go back to being the same old Zoe. Even if her wish for love didn't come true, she had a brighter future ahead of her than the one she'd dreamed of.

She had Sean to thank.

Because he had believed in her, depended on her, she could believe in and depend on herself.

Tears pricked the corners of her eyes.

Even if he didn't need her anymore.

A noise sounded behind her.

Uh-oh. Someone had found her favorite hiding spot. No doubt her mother or one of her brothers.

"I'll go back inside," she said, not turning. "I just needed some fresh air."

"Don't rush back on my account."

The familiar male voice sent her pulse racing. She turned slowly, afraid she was imagining things.

But she wasn't.

Her heart leapt. "You're here."

Dressed in a black tux and looking devastatingly handsome, he made his way toward her on crutches. "You look gorgeous, absolutely stunning, like a real-life princess in that gown. Though I must admit to being partial to you in wet, clingy pajamas."

Zoe's heart melted at the compliment, but she forced herself to straighten. "Aren't you supposed to be at the Rail Jam Extravaganza?"

"I sent two of my employees who I'm sure will rise to the occasion," he said. "You're my top priority, Zoe."

The air rushed from her lungs. No one had ever said those words to her before.

Standing in front of her, he tucked a piece of hair behind her ear, the gesture so tender her eyes stung. "For years, I've told myself I didn't have time for a relationship. I wouldn't listen to my family, to anyone. Then you came along, and all I could see, want, dream about was you. I should have never let you leave. I'm sorry, Zoe. I should have believed you when you told me who you were. Not Zoe Carrington or Zoe Flynn. Just Zoe. But I was too stubborn to realize it."

She swallowed, hoping to find her voice. "I'm sorry, too. I should have trusted you with the truth, Sean, but so many times people I've known have run to the tabloids to make a quick buck…"

"We both should have done a lot of things."

Her heart bumped. "All I've ever wanted is to be loved and accepted for who I am. Not what my family or friends expect. I just want to be me. I'm not going to settle for anything less."

"I don't want you to settle." Sean held her hand. "I love you. Only you."

The sincerity in Sean's eyes and voice told Zoe his words were true. She smiled. "I love you."

"Do you think we could try again?" he asked. "I want to take you back to Hood Hamlet, back home."

Her heart fluttered. "I'd like that."

Sean lowered his mouth, pressing his sweet lips upon hers. He swept Zoe against him with one arm, her skin tingling where he touched her.

His lips moved over hers. Tasting. Caressing. Loving.

She melted into the kiss, drinking up the taste of him. His warmth and his strength danced through her veins.

Zoe gave in to his passion, returning his kiss with a desire all her own. She didn't know how long they stood there, how long they kissed. The only thing that mattered was this time. This man. This love.

Slowly, with a heartrending tenderness, Sean drew the kiss to an end.

Zoe stared at the man she loved. The affection in his eyes matched the way she felt in her heart. Every kiss, every touch they'd shared had brought them to this moment. "So you're going to be my real-life boyfriend."

He shook his head, a quick, decisive gesture that stopped her heart.

"I want to be more than your boyfriend. We've had only one official date, but being with you these past weeks has shown me it will work. I want you to know I'm committed." Sean swung backward, tried to move, then stopped. "Damn crutches."

She let go of the breath she'd been holding. "What?"

"I can't go down on one knee because of my leg, so this will have to do. Marry me, Zoe Flynn Carrington. Be my wife. Be my partner. Be my everything."

This was everything she imagined it would be and more. Joy overflowed. "I'd be honored to be your wife, Sean. Yes. Yes, I'll marry you."

Inside, the people started counting down to midnight.

He pulled out a velvet ring box, opened it up and, as the

horns blared the ringing-in of a new year, slid the ring onto Zoe's finger. A perfect fit.

She gazed at the intricate filigree and diamonds, a feeling of family and home and tradition welling up inside her. "Your grandmother's ring?"

He nodded. "We seem to have been fated from that first day we met, but if you don't like it—"

"I love it," she said. "But not as much as I love you."

Sean grinned. "Happy New Year, Zoe."

He brushed his lips across hers once more.

A feeling of contentment flowed through her. It was as if this was the moment she'd been waiting for, but it wasn't the ending. Only the beginning.

"Happy New Year, my love," she said.

Zoe stared up at Sean with stars in her eyes and his ring on her finger. She smiled. There had been some Christmas magic left after all.

Coming Next Month

Available December 7, 2010

REQUEST YOUR FREE BOOKS!
2 FREE NOVELS PLUS 2
FREE GIFTS!

HARLEQUIN® *Romance.*

From the Heart, For the Heart

YES! Please send me 2 FREE Harlequin® Romance novels and my 2 FREE gifts (gifts are worth about $10). After receiving them, if I don't wish to receive any more books, I can return the shipping statement marked "cancel." If I don't cancel, I will receive 6 brand-new novels every month and be billed just $3.84 per book in the U.S. or $4.24 per book in Canada. That's a savings of 15% off the cover price! It's quite a bargain! Shipping and handling is just 50¢ per book.* I understand that accepting the 2 free books and gifts places me under no obligation to buy anything. I can always return a shipment and cancel at any time. Even if I never buy another book from Harlequin, the two free books and gifts are mine to keep forever.

116/316 HDN E7T2

Name _____ (PLEASE PRINT)

Address _____ Apt. #

City _____ State/Prov. _____ Zip/Postal Code

Signature (if under 18, a parent or guardian must sign)

Mail to the **Harlequin Reader Service:**
IN U.S.A.: P.O. Box 1867, Buffalo, NY 14240-1867
IN CANADA: P.O. Box 609, Fort Erie, Ontario L2A 5X3

Not valid for current subscribers to Harlequin Romance books.

**Are you a subscriber to Harlequin Romance books
and want to receive the larger-print edition?
Call 1-800-873-8635 or visit www.ReaderService.com.**

* Terms and prices subject to change without notice. Prices do not include applicable taxes. Sales tax applicable in N.Y. Canadian residents will be charged applicable provincial taxes and GST. Offer not valid in Quebec. This offer is limited to one order per household. All orders subject to approval. Credit or debit balances in a customer's account(s) may be offset by any other outstanding balance owed by or to the customer. Please allow 4 to 6 weeks for delivery. Offer available while quantities last.

Your Privacy: Harlequin Books is committed to protecting your privacy. Our Privacy Policy is available online at www.ReaderService.com or upon request from the Reader Service. From time to time we make our lists of customers available to reputable third parties who may have a product or service of interest to you. If you would prefer we not share your name and address, please check here. ☐

Help us get it right—We strive for accurate, respectful and relevant communications. To clarify or modify your communication preferences, visit us at www.ReaderService.com/consumerschoice.

HR10R2

HARLEQUIN®

A Romance

FOR EVERY MOOD™

Spotlight on
Classic

Quintessential, modern love stories
that are romance at its finest.

See the next page
to enjoy a sneak peek from
the Harlequin® Romance series.

*See below for a sneak peek from our classic
Harlequin® Romance® line.*

Introducing DADDY BY CHRISTMAS by Patricia Thayer.

MIA caught sight of Jarrett when he walked into the open lobby. It was hard not to notice the man. In a charcoal business suit with a crisp white shirt and striped tie covered by a dark trench coat, he looked more Wall Street than small-town Colorado.

Mia couldn't blame him for keeping his distance. He was probably tired of taking care of her.

Besides, why would a man like Jarrett McKane be interested in her? Why would he want to take on a woman expecting a baby? Yet he'd done so many things for her. He'd been there when she'd needed him most. How could she not care about a man like that?

Heart pounding in her ears, she walked up behind him. Jarrett turned to face her. "Did you get enough sleep last night?"

"Yes, thanks to you," she said, wondering if he'd thought about their kiss. Her gaze went to his mouth, then she quickly glanced away. "And thank you for not bringing up my meltdown."

Jarrett couldn't stop looking at Mia. Blue was definitely her color, bringing out the richness of her eyes.

"What meltdown?" he said, trying hard to focus on what she was saying. "You were just exhausted from lack of sleep and worried about your baby."

He couldn't help remembering how, during the night, he'd kept going in to watch her sleep. How strange was that? "I hope you got enough rest."

She nodded. "Plenty. And you're a good neighbor for

coming to my rescue."

He tensed. Neighbor? *What neighbor kisses you like I did?* "That's me, just the full-service landlord," he said, trying to keep the sarcasm out of his voice. He started to leave, but she put her hand on his arm.

"Jarrett, what I meant was you went beyond helping me." Her eyes searched his face. "I've asked far too much of you."

"Did you hear me complain?"

She shook her head. "You should. I feel like I've taken advantage."

"Like I said, I haven't minded."

"And I'm grateful for everything…"

Grasping her hand on his arm, Jarrett leaned forward. The memory of last night's kiss had him aching for another. "I didn't do it for your gratitude, Mia."

Gorgeous tycoon Jarrett McKane has never believed in Christmas—but he can't help being drawn to soon-to-be-mom Mia Saunders! Christmases past were spent alone…and now Jarrett may just have a fairy-tale ending for all his Christmases future!

*Available December 2010,
only from Harlequin® Romance®.*

HARLEQUIN *Presents*

Bestselling Harlequin Presents® author

Julia James

brings you her most powerful book yet…

FORBIDDEN OR FOR BEDDING?

The shamed mistress…

Guy de Rochemont's name is a byword for wealth
and power—and now his duty is to wed.

Alexa Harcourt knows she can never be anything
more than *The de Rochemont Mistress*.

But Alexa—the one woman Guy wants—is also
the one woman whose reputation
forbids him to take her as his wife….

**Available from Harlequin Presents
December 2010**

www.eHarlequin.com

HP12960